Poets and Piracy

Mission 3 of the
BLACK OCEAN
Series

J.S. Morin

Poets and Piracy
Mission 3 of: Black Ocean

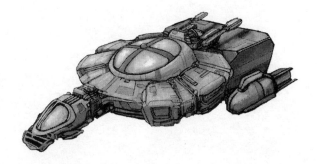

The crew of the *Mobius*:

Bradley Carlin "Carl" Ramsey (Human, Male, 32): Captain of the *Mobius*. Former starfighter pilot who left Earth Navy under questionable circumstances. Smuggler and petty con man with a love of ancient rock music.

Tania Louise "Tanny" Ramsey (Human, Female, 31): Pilot of the *Mobius*. Former marine drop-ship pilot and Carl's ex-wife. Daughter of a notorious crime lord who joined the marines to get away from her family.

Mordecai "Mort" The Brown (Human, Male, 52): Ship's wizard. On the run from the Convocation, he serves in place of the *Mobius'* shoddy, star-drive. "The" is his legal middle name, a tradition in the Brown family.

Rodek of Kethlet "Roddy" (Laaku, Male, 45): Ship's mechanic. Laaku are a quadridexterous race with prehensile feet, evolved from a species similar to the chimpanzees of Earth. Never to be found without a beer in hand, he keeps the cobbled-together *Mobius* running.

Mriy Yrris (Azrin, Female, 16): Ship's security. The azrin are felid race who still hunt for their food. Despite her lethargy and slouching posture, she is a ferocious warrior.

Esper Theresa Richelieu (Human, Female, 24): Former initiate priestess of the One Church. She tried to do the right thing the wrong way, and it cost her a place in the hierarchy. Though she's signed on with the *Mobius*, she's still not sure what role fits her best.

Kubu (Species Unknown, Male, Age Unknown): A sentient dog-like creature, rescued from an illegal zoo.

Tanny popped the pills into her mouth in little squadrons. Two blues and a pink. A yellow with black stripe, a squarish red, and a clear amber. Four clean white ones shaped like torpedoes. A pair of chalky hexagons and a trio of half-brown, half-yellow capsules. The last to go was a single pill in a metallic casing, printed with a red letter R in gothic script and a standard ARGO hazard marker. She chased each swallow with a mouthful of ginger soda, both to settle her stomach and to kill the bitter aftertaste from the chalky pills. The whole conglomeration fizzed and churned in her stomach as they set out on their assigned tasks.

Centrimac boosted her immune system. A constant presence of it in her system had kept her from so much as a sniffle since she joined the marines. Carl and Roddy came down with something every second or third trip planetside, but not Tanny. She had heard that it took the edge off a hangover too, but she wasn't about to abstain to check for herself.

Plexophan improved her balance and reflexes. There was some weird enzyme in it developed by the yishar that altered her muscle fibers. They no longer used the same chemical process as most humans. Once she had tried research how that all worked, but no explanation made sense unless you had a degree in biochemistry—preferably an advanced one, focused on xenobiology.

Adrenophiline altered adrenaline production and consumption in the body. Any marine with a year's service had adrenal glands twice the size he enlisted with, and they replenished at six times the normal rate. It also eased the jittery feeling that came after the rush wore off.

A few of the pills were simple mineral supplements. Most humans didn't need a lot of molybdenum, selenium, or cobalt, but anyone with a daily regimen like Tanny's required them. The identical white pills were compacted mixes of auto-release hormones, designed to keep her mood level—she had never found them that effective, but she was worse off without them.

Some of the drugs were just included to cancel out side effects of the others. Plexophan increased her metabolism, but also spiked her appetite out of proportion to the increase. Pseudoanorex counteracted that effect, but resulted in lightheadedness that Zygrana balanced out. Cannabinol was there to reduce the anxiety and nausea that Adrenophiline induced.

The centerpiece of the whole cocktail was Recitol, which saturated every marine's system. Though the drug's maker used a soft C sound in the recipient-care video, the marine nickname "Wreck-It-All" came to be the more common pronunciation. It allowed the body to use quick, efficient bursts of adrenaline at will, hyper-oxygenated the blood, and slowed the perception of time by an estimated 11 to 12 percent. It also suppressed activity in the ventrolateral frontal cortex, the part of the brain responsible for morality and conscience. Tanny had been taking Sepromax to counteract the latter effect since re-entering civilian life, but she was unwilling to give up the other benefits.

The water from the faucet shocked Tanny alert as she splashed her face. Leaning heavily on the sides of the sink, she watched her reflection in the mirror. Staring into her own eyes, she waited until the stranger lurking there faded away and she could connect the image with a sense of self.

The scrawled red lines receded until the whites were clear; the pupils contracted in reaction to the glare of the mirror light. There was a knock at the door. "What?" she snapped. It hadn't been an invitation, but the door opened anyway.

"Sorry," Esper said. The hangdog expression and the apologetic duck drained the venom from Tanny. Suddenly embarrassed, she reached over and snapped shut the case where she kept her pills. "*What was that?*" Esper never said it aloud, but her furrowed brow and the tilt of her head to get a better look said it for her.

"What?" Tanny repeated, holding the case behind her. The Adrenophiline must still have been digging its claws into her brain. She rationalized that if anyone on the *Mobius* was incapable of threatening her, it was Esper. With a conscious effort, she set the case down on the side of the sink and dared Esper to ask about its contents.

"Roddy sent me," Esper said. "It's Kubu. Roddy says there is 2.6 kilos of sub-grade fertilizer in the hold. He says if you don't clean it up, he's delivering it."

"Like to see him try," Tanny muttered.

"... through the faucet," Esper added.

Tanny glanced to the sink and the churning froth in her stomach soured. The last thing she needed was to vomit up a thousand terras worth of marine biochemicals. Recitol was a weekly, and there weren't many pills left in her stash. She wasn't ready to go without until she could buy more.

Esper seemed to notice her discomfort. "He didn't *actually* do it ... yet."

"I'm surprised he didn't make you clean it up," Tanny said. "Aren't you his assistant these days?"

"Not today," Esper replied. "I've just been in and out of the hold, moving stuff from the conference room. I'm converting it to passenger quarters so we can make actual money on fares. Carl and Roddy both seemed pretty keen on the idea, so—"

"Fine," Tanny snapped. She didn't need an affidavit. It was a simple enough question. "I'll get right down there."

Once the door closed behind Esper, Tanny reopened the pill case. Supplies were always hit or miss. Sometimes she'd find a dealer with a glut of Plexophan, or a fence would have a load of boosted Recitol. It was rare to find things in balanced ratios to match her regimen. Since her recent change to a higher dose of Sepromax, she had run her reserves dangerously low, and a few other pills weren't far behind.

An hour of cross-referencing the itinerary of the *Mobius* (a work of optimistic fiction at the best of times) against known gray-market pharmacists, Tanny concluded that she wasn't going to stumble across anyone who had what she needed. Her finger hovered over the button for the intra-ship comm as she decided whether she could afford to wait and hope to get lucky along the way, or if she really needed to make this particular call. Deciding that withdrawal symptoms were worse than asking for help, she closed her eyes and pressed.

"Yo!" Carl's voice came through from his quarters. "To what do I owe the—"

"I'm running low," Tanny blurted before Carl could get any farther.

The flippant joviality was gone. "Esper came by and mentioned you were a bit worn thin. I told her not to worry. How low we talkin'?"

"A week," Tanny replied. "I'd feel better with four days, plus some wiggle room."

"Gotcha," Carl replied. He sounded relieved. "We can reroute to Tau Ceti. Ought to be plenty of options there." Why did he have to be so goddamn understanding? He'd tried to get her to detox more times than she could count. Tanny had hoped he'd be put out, that he'd argue with her about it again, that he actually cared where they were headed and found a detour inconvenient.

But once again, Carl was just going to have them drop everything and head off to find her a seller. All she could think to say was, "Thanks."

The first day of their side trip to Tau Ceti IV was winding to a close as Esper and Roddy returned to the *Mobius*. Her borrowed datapad was filled with items and their associated prices from their day's window-shopping. Esper held the screen so that the laaku mechanic could follow along as she explained her vision. "There's plenty of room for a washroom, mini fridge/food-processor combo, and a holo-projector, not to mention a bed, dresser, and all that other stuff. A tiny hotel room right here on the *Mobius*."

Roddy rolled his eyes. Esper was meant to notice, but she deigned not to acknowledge. She continued delving into details of plumbing fixtures and upholstery as they made their way through the cargo bay. But when Roddy opened the door to the common room, their conversation stopped abruptly as a wall of deafening noise from the holo-projector drowned them out.

Unlike most of the ancient fare that cluttered up the computer core, Esper recognized this one from the promotional vids from a few years back. She couldn't recall the name, but it was a Zach Spanner military-action vid. They were all alike, as near as she could tell; some misfit pilot nearly gets his squad killed—or he does get them killed early on and he's the only survivor—and loses his confidence, only to save the day in the third act. In the holographic field, little generic enemy spacecraft were blowing up at a mind-boggling rate as the hero spouted patriotic jeers at them—as if it were their fault for not being born human.

Carl sat slumped on the couch, watching the action with dead eyes. By his side, Mort appeared to be in much better spirits, munching on cheese-drizzled chips as he took in the show.

"Lousy fuckers," Roddy griped loudly enough to be heard over an exploding ship. "You loaded up *Last Stand at Zulu Seven* without me?"

Mort elbowed Carl in the ribs, and it roused him enough to pause the vid. The din ebbed to background levels. "Don't worry about it," Mort replied. "We can watch it again later. His eyes are open, but nothing's getting in."

"Yeah," Roddy replied, pointing at the frozen hologram. "But now I know how it's going to end."

Mort scoffed. "If you don't know how it's going to end, you haven't watched *Last Stand at Luna, Last Stand at Daedalus Colony,* or *Last Stand of Miracle Squadron.*"

Esper studied Carl as he slouched. It was unlike him to remain silent. He wasn't normally the sort to let a conversation happen without him. "What's wrong with Carl?"

"Oh, that's right. You're still new around here," Mort said. "You're familiar with Carl the Starship Captain, Carl the Swindler, and Carl the Cocksure Ex-Fighter Pilot. You might even have met Carl the Drunken Ladies' Man, though that's none of my business. Well ..." He bracketed Carl with his outstretched hands, "Meet Carl the Just Lost All His Money at Poker."

"*All* his money?" Esper asked.

"Bullshit," Roddy muttered.

"He was smart enough to pre-pay his tram fare round-trip, or we would've had to send someone to get him," Mort replied.

"How'd we let him wander off on his own again?" Roddy asked.

Mort shrugged. "We'd already split the take from the Hadrian advance. It's *his* money he lost."

"And the ship fund?" Roddy asked. "I'm the one who has to deal with this bucket on no budget."

"Paid the fuel guy before I left," Carl muttered.

"Oh, so you're not catatonic over there, gamblin' man?" Roddy asked. "I spend the whole goddamn day trying to keep Esper's hotel idea below cost so there'd be enough left over to overhaul the power plant. We've beaten that poor thing to hell."

"So ... what?" Esper asked, waving the datapad. "We can't put in passenger quarters now?"

"Not unless we're converting the ping-pong table into a bunk," Roddy replied.

The scrabbling of approaching claws carried through the door to the cargo hold. Seconds later, the door opened and Kubu bounded through, followed by Tanny. He leaped onto the couch and forced himself between Carl and Mort, curling into a ball.

"I take it he didn't like the university?" Esper asked.

"I swear this animal is bigger than when you left with him," Mort said, edging away from the furry mass.

"I left him there a couple hours while they did some intelligence testing on him," Tanny replied. She raised an eyebrow at Kubu. "Apparently, he's not brain damaged, this is normal for whatever he is."

"Still no idea what species this sack of muscle is?" Roddy asked.

"That Dunkirk guy is still working on it," Tanny replied. "We might not have an answer by the time we drop out of here, so I left him a comm ID where he could contact me."

Roddy grunted. "Chip was always good for a secure false comm ID. You gonna be clean?"

"The guy's a university professor," Tanny replied. "What's he going to do?"

Just then a muffled chime emanated from Carl's pocket. It was an unfamiliar melody, but it sounded like one of Carl's classical rock pieces, with scratchy guitars making the lyrics incomprehensible. He dug a datapad from inside his jacket. "Knock it off, everyone," he said. "Unknown ID. Shit." He answered the call. "Hey, who you looking for?"

Whoever was on the other end of the connection was too quiet for Esper to hear.

"I might be," he answered. "Who told you that?... Never heard of him. ... Yeah, yeah, sure... You got a name?... Hope you don't mind me checking up on that ID... No, that's not a problem. ... Depends. How soon you need us there?... No, I'd rather work out those details in person. There's only so far I'm trusting this comm link. ... All right. It's a deal."

Carl shut down the datapad and slipped it back inside his jacket. "Which one of you was blabbing?"

He had asked the room at large, but his eyes were on Esper. "Why are you looking at me?"

"Tanny, did you happen to mention to anyone that we were getting into the passenger business?" Carl asked. She shook her head. "How about you, Mort?"

"I was bowling," Mort said. "Found a few lanes in the arcanopolis in Stevenston. Just a bunch of Order of Gaia blowhards. I could have flat out told them I was a Convocation fugitive and they'd have brushed it off. None of them have been off-world in his life, and most probably couldn't work a comm."

"How about you, Roddy? You go bar-hopping and spill our plans?"

"Piss off," Roddy replied. "I was with Miss Baroque here, picking out bed linens and furniture."

Esper gave a sheepish smile. "Maybe Mriy…"

"She's hiking," Carl replied. "And she's *such* a gossip, especially to people who can't understand azrin."

Roddy squinted up at Esper. "Wait a minute. You told them what we were outfitting, didn't you?"

Esper held up her hands. "Just the appliance salesman and the woman at the store where we found the bed I wanted. It was easier than trying to explain all the corridors we had to transport things through and the layout of the conference room. Once they knew it was a modified turtledove-class shuttle—"

"Wait, you told them we were a chop-ship?" Tanny asked.

"That explains how they ID'ed us, at least," Carl said, nodding to himself. "Someone in one of those stores did some digging and found a non-standard turtledove that landed recently. Not exactly astral cartography. It's beside the point now, anyway. Someone wants to hire us."

"I figured that much from your half of the conversation," Tanny said. "What's the job?"

"Passenger transport," Carl replied. "Pickup is in-system on Drei, one of Tau Ceti VII's moons. Drop-off details to be provided in person."

"That's a rough neighborhood," Tanny said.

"I imagine that's why they wanted someone like us."

"Hold on a minute," Esper said. "Since it seems to be something we need to ask around here, *who* are we transporting? We running slaves, kidnapped witnesses, escaped inmates ... am I getting warm?" After the incident at the Gologlex Menagerie, she felt the need to get the unpleasantries out in the open up front.

"It was the guy on the comm," Carl said. "Can't promise he hasn't escaped from anywhere, but he gave me an ID to run a background on him. Either he's clean or has a nice forged ID."

"Who's gonna run that background?" Roddy asked. By his tone, it wasn't going to be him.

Carl just shrugged. "Wasn't going to bother. Chip might have cracked a false ID, but no one here can do better than taking whatever bait he left us. I'll dig up the basics on the omni, just to see what he looks like."

Mort cleared his throat. "Where's he going to sleep?"

"Shit," Carl muttered as he threw his head back against the couch cushions.

❀ ❀ ❀

Tau Ceti VII had three moons, all terraformed: Einer, Zwei, and Drei; none was the sort of place that drew vacationers from far-flung systems. It was a hazard of being one of the first systems humans colonized; terramancers were more than willing to stick close to home and keep making every orbital body habitable, rather than traipse across the galaxy. Despite its potato-like shape, Drei was a warren of cities connected by tramway tunnels, clinging to a breathable atmosphere.

All the landing bays were of Port-of-St.Paul enclosed, which was just as well, because the air quality on the moon was notoriously rough on non-natives. As Carl stepped off the cargo ramp, he stumbled in the gravity change. Here and there you'd find an inhabited world with as much as a 10 percent variance from Earth's gravity, but moons threw a lot of those rules out the airlock. Drei had less than half of Earth Standard, and every organ in Carl's body shifted under the new, lesser pull.

"I hate that," he muttered. "Why can't you people just fix that shit when these moons get terraformed?"

Mort snorted. He strode past the bounding Carl as if the moon's gravity wasn't affecting him any differently. "Just ignore it. Besides, they built this place centuries ago. I doubt the locals would take kindly to anyone mucking about with their little worldlet. Locals are funny like that. Consistent too. Just about anything you'd like to fix is some sort of offense. Nasty buggers, locals."

"No, Kubu," Tanny said, holding the dog at bay. "Stay." Kubu was having no part of being left behind, trying to force his way past Tanny to follow Carl.

Carl turned back, regretting the sudden motion while his mind and body were still struggling to assimilate to the gravity shift. "Maybe you should just stay on board. It's not like we can't handle this ourselves. Besides, Kubu might get into just about anything."

"I'm not a dog-sitter," Tanny snapped, despite having her arm wrapped around Kubu's chest in a wrestling hold.

"Hey, he's your responsibility."

Tanny fumed, but Roddy hit the release to raise the cargo ramp. Ex-wife, mechanic, and dog all disappeared from view.

"The dark beast shall be the death of us all," Mort said, his voice dry and sepulchral.

Carl shied away from him. "Was that supposed to be some sort of prophecy?"

Mort just snickered, his shoulders shaking gently. "Nah, I imagine the overgrown slipper-chewer will grow out of it. Tanny's just in for a rough go of it in the meantime."

"I didn't know you knew anything about dogs."

"What's to know? Simplest creatures on Earth. Probably simplest creatures on whatever planet Kubu's from. Not a bit of guile or malice in them."

"Well, odds are this guy we're meeting has plenty of both," Carl said. They walked from the hangar area into the public section of the spaceport. There were the usual shops and cafés, as if someone designing a spaceport figured anyone new planetside needed a memento shirt or a cup of overpriced coffee. The central hub of the plaza featured a decorative fountain with sprays and jets of water that drifted in the low gravity to catch offworlders' attention.

"What kind of a name is that, anyway? Bryce Brisson?" Mort asked. "It has to be a fake."

"Could be," Carl agreed. "Or maybe his parents just hated him. Didn't do him any favors in life, if any of that bio is real. He's done time—nothing major. A couple cons, a hold-up, shit that'd get you dusted on Earth but only a couple years' cold time in the borderlands."

"Wash the suds off the notion that any of that poppycock is worth a damn," Mort said. "Want to know if a man's a phony? Look him in the eye. All a matter of observation and a keen understanding of the mind."

"Try me," Carl said.

"Anyone *else*."

"Well, we're going to be in for a lot more keen looks into guy's eyes if we don't find another tech juggler," Carl said. "I've been thinking of asking Esper to take a course over the omni."

"Whoa there, cowboy," Mort said, holding up both hands and waggling them. "I like that girl. Got a head between those ears of hers. In all the time you've had the *Mobius*, we haven't kept anyone in that job who hasn't either come to a bad end or stuck a knife in us when time came to share the spoils of our own cleverness."

Carl sighed. It was an old argument, but he pulled on his verbal boxing gloves once again. "It's all a matter of coincidence. There's nothing to say Esper will have anything bad happen to her just because she knows how to wrangle a computer core or slog through the muck in the back alleys of omni. And can you honestly picture her turning on us? She won't even fire a blaster at a target dummy that's shaped like a human."

"We're damn fools if we let her," Mort replied. "Time and again the universe tells us we're not supposed to muck around with that garbage. How many times do you have to burn your hand to stop sticking it in the fire?"

"Maybe this Bryce guy will be a computer Einstein," Carl said. "We can have him run a check on his own fake ID."

Mort sighed. "You're doing that mocking little sing-song thing again. I win the argument."

"Fuck you and your argument rules! The universe is *not* trying to send me a personal message about who I can hire for my crew."

Mort grunted. "Where are we supposed to find this mystery passenger?" The two of them passed the ChuggaGuzzle that marked the end of the shopping area. Overhead signage pointed out various outlets into the surrounding city of Tangiers Gamma.

"I wanted to scout this place out for a good meet-up spot and send him a comm." Carl took a moment to glance at his options and headed in the direction of the Galveston District. The subheading mentioned industrial processing, ore refinery, and freight transfer—not the sort of place many people would go by accident.

"So, we're just wandering?"

Carl took a bounding step and turned in mid-air to face Mort. "For now."

Mort glared sidelong at Carl, and might have raised some objection, had not someone beaten him to it. "Sir, if you'll step aside please," a helmet-muffled voice addressed Carl.

Two uniformed security officers separated themselves from the crowd and barred Carl and Mort's path. Behind the helms, they probably bore distinguishing features, but with the darkened visors, gloved hands, and regulation law-enforcement physique, it was impossible to tell one from the other.

"Sorry fellas; there must be some mistake," Carl said with an easy smile. It was a reflex. He hadn't given any thought to the response. "We just got here."

"Get back to us in an hour, maybe two if we're slow," Mort added. That was when Carl knew the wizard was thinking along with him. They weren't going quietly.

The security officer tapped a finger on the side of his visor. "You are Captain Bradley Carlin Ramsey of the Earth-registered ship *Mobius*. There is a warrant for your arrest for an incident that took place on Orion Station Echo Nine. Please place your hands on your head."

Carl blinked in disbelief. His first instinct had been that Bryce Brisson had set him up. But this was legit. Someone with too much time on his hands had put together enough pieces to dump the mayhem on Echo Nine at his feet. The paltry blaster pistols in the officers' hands had every right to be aimed his way. From his vantage, Carl couldn't tell whether they were set to stun. If Mort wasn't quick, that little detail might make all the difference. Trusting that this wasn't a "he was reaching for a weapon" setup, Carl complied. The stream of factory workers and freight handlers that had filled the corridor a minute earlier dispersed with guilty haste, as if they all wanted to dissociate themselves from whatever Carl had done.

"I'm sure we can work something—"

There was a minor tremor in the air, and a sound like a faulty compressor coil just before it burnt out. One of the security guards dropped to the floor like dead weight. The tremor and sound repeated, and this time Carl saw the blue of the stun bolt just as it struck the second guard and sent him limply to the ground as well.

The man with the stun pistol in his hand looked familiar, just like his flatpic on the omni. Bryce Brisson wore a comm headset with the mic flipped away from his face, and carried a travel pack over one shoulder. "I'd hoped to meet under less urgent circumstances, but we can work out a payment once we're off this rock."

"Um, thanks," Carl said, his fingers still laced together, resting on his head.

"This is our fare?" Mort asked.

"You boys always this slow?" Bryce asked, waving the stun pistol in a beckoning gesture toward the hangars. "We've gotta get out of here."

Carl opened his mouth. Words were about to come out—something protesting the presumption on the part of one Bryce Brisson, prospective passenger. But there were two stunned security officers on the ground at his feet, and enough witnesses that there was a good chance one might decide he didn't have amnesia and ID Carl and Mort. The words on the tip of Carl's tongue transformed. "We've got to stash these guys."

"We can shove them in there," Mort said, pointing to a nearby door labeled "Grade Epsilon Clearance Required."

"Hacking that will take more time than we've—" Bryce began, but he stopped himself mid-sentence. Mort had already made his way to the door. With none of the wizardly trappings of spellcasting, he simply jammed a finger into the key-card reader. The metal of the device glowed red as Mort's finger pushed through, and the innards crackled and sparked in their death throes. The door popped open.

"Give me a hand," Bryce said to Carl, reaching down to grab hold of one of the security guards. Before he could reach the limp form, both guards slid along the floor, pulled by an unseen force.

"No time for mucking around with grunt work," Mort said. "And since we're past the point of subtlety ..." He muttered something guttural and pointed a finger down the corridor and upward. A gout of flame spilled forth from empty air, setting off alarms and sending the remaining bystanders scattering.

"Holy shit," Bryce said, throwing an arm up to shield his face.

"You're with us, I guess," Carl said. "Come on."

The run was awkward in the low gravity. Carl bounded along with Bryce as his heels. Mort outpaced them, taking advantage of being able selectively ignore the effects of gravity on his creaky old carcass.

"Can you call ahead to your ship?" Bryce asked, huffing as he ran.

Carl broke stride to fish his comm from his jacket pocket. He hit the transmit button, but the device failed to respond. "Nope," he replied. "Mort blew my comm with his little tantrum."

"You should have mentioned wanting to call the ship sooner," Mort said.

"Half the responders in the city are going to be heading this way to deal with that fire," Bryce said. "I was counting on us having a few minutes' head start before anyone knew what was going on."

"We still ... have it," Carl replied, beginning to feel the effects of a sedentary life aboard ship. The run was wearing on him already. A hover-shuttle headed their way bearing four red-garbed emergency personnel in full environmental protective gear, faces hidden behind breather helmets. "Fire! Back ... that way!" Carl shouted to them, pointing the direction they had come from. As soon as they were past, he slowed to a walk, then stopped. "Hold up. They're dealing with a fire, not us. Play this cool and we get back to the *Mobius* like nothing happened."

Mort slowed to match his pace. "Good enough for me. I'm too old for shit like this. What do you think they'll have done to keep us from flying off?"

"Probably a no-fly order to traffic control," Carl replied, still breathing heavily. "There's nothing between us and the Black Ocean, though; this is a moon, not a sealed station. We're likely to get patrol craft after us."

They entered the plaza, which looked like a different world with the chaos of commerce and idle snacking replaced by the chaos of fire response teams coming and everyone else fleeing for cover.

"Leave that to me," Bryce replied. "I've got claws in local computer systems. I can get them seeing false images on their sensors, enough to throw them off for an escape."

Oh, really? Carl remembered Chip saying something like that once. It had worked, but Carl had written off having that sort of technical help on board since Chip's death. Maybe this Bryce was worth more than just a paying fare. "Bryce, you carrying your fare in that pack by any chance?"

"Captain Ramsey, I'm carrying all my worldly possessions in this pack," Bryce replied.

"Good, because we still have to work out a payment for this trip of yours."

"Maybe now's not the best time to be negotiating," Bryce said.

"Look," Carl said. "We're about five minutes—maybe six—from blasting off this rock with a whole freighter of trouble left in our wake. If you don't want to be the one to clean it up, I think you're going to take whatever I offer."

"You're bluffing," Bryce said. "You wouldn't risk having half the planetary defense force after you."

"If there's one thing my crew can tell you: I never know when to back off a bluff. Your fare is that pack of yours and everything in it, and I'm guessing it's still not going to cover the fallout from this shit supernova."

"Anyone ever tell you you're an ass?" Bryce asked. When Carl just grinned in reply, he relented. "Deal."

The *Mobius* was still waiting for them when they got to the hangar. All along the retreat, Carl had a nagging worry that there would be an armed security unit waiting there for him, with an impounded ship and his crew already taken into custody. The cargo bay door lowered as they approached, and Roddy gave the fleeing trio a wave.

"Didn't expect you guys back so soon," he shouted across the hangar bay. "This our guy?"

"Fire up the engines," Carl called back. "Comm Tanny and tell her if she's not in the cockpit by the time I get there, I'm flying."

"We in some kind of—"

"NOW!"

"Sure thing, boss-man," Roddy replied. He hit the comm panel by the cargo bay door. Carl couldn't hear what he said, but Roddy held up his hands in a placating gesture that was lost on Tanny at the other end of the conversation. Apparently Carl's impromptu departure was an inconvenience.

A minute later, Carl, Mort, and Bryce were in the common room. Mort collapsed onto the couch, while Bryce stood with one hand on the strap of his pack, looking lost. "Where can I get a good signal?"

"Cockpit," Carl replied. "With me. Mort, you get ready to take us astral."

"Wait ... the wizard's doing it?" Bryce asked with a rising note of panic. "No offense, but I assumed you people used a star drive. I didn't sign on for—"

"I didn't sign on for any of this," Carl snapped. There was a telltale shift in the feel of the floor beneath his feet. The subtle shift in engine vibration meant that they had just cleared the ground. "We're past the point of leaving you behind. So suck it up and trust us to get you out of here ... our way."

Carl strode down the corridor to the cockpit. En route they passed the converted conference room. The door was open, and Esper was waiting inside, but there was no time for her just then. "Carl, what's—" she began, but Carl was already past the doorway and she let the question drop.

"Tanny, what've we got?" Carl asked as he leaned over the co-pilot's seat.

"How about you tell *me* that?" Tanny sniped back. "Where are we even heading?"

"They were waiting for us with a warrant," Carl replied. "Just plot us a course anywhere extra-solar. We'll worry about navigation once we're astral. Oh, and watch out for planetary security. By the way, this is Bryce. Bryce, Tanny. Tanny, Bryce Brisson."

"Where can I interface?" Bryce asked.

Carl stepped aside and allowed Bryce into the co-pilot's seat. "Work it."

"What's he—?"

Carl didn't let Tanny finish. "He's putting enough ships on the planetary sensor net that we can slip away in the confusion. I guess he's good at that sort of thing."

Bryce fished a device from his pack that looked like a miniature computer core. He took a cable that sprouted from one end of it and scanned the ship's main console until he found a matching port. "Give me a few seconds to get connected, and ... what the ...?" He gave the portable core a firm whack and squinted at the display. "It's dead."

"We're dead," Tanny said matter-of-factly. The *Mobius* was picking up five patrol class closing on their location. She looked up at Carl and shook her head in disgust. "You're as good with techies as you are with cards."

Carl scanned the sensor displays. They had chosen Port-of-St.Paul for its relatively remote location, so there was some slop in the patrol response window. "We've got time. Get us to orbit and park just out of atmo." He hit the comm. "Roddy, get the shields ready to take a pounding." Keying off the comm, he rushed from the cockpit.

"Where you going?" Tanny asked.

"To make Mort's day."

❁ ❁ ❁

Esper sat on the couch with her hands folded in her lap. She had fled there after Carl and their new passenger flew past the guest quarters. Something was wrong, she had realized, and Mort had confirmed her suspicion. The wizard sat beside her, leaning forward to rest elbows on his knees.

Footsteps pounded down the corridor toward them, culminating in Carl's breathless entrance. "Mort, I need you to be ready. Drop us... soon as I say."

"How deep?" Mort asked.

"*Bury* us."

A glint flickered in Mort's eye as he replied. "As you command, Lord Ramsey."

Carl gave him a raised eyebrow. "Don't go archaic on me. Just get us astral enough that planetary security can't fire on us." He held up a palm to calm Mort's manic look, then headed back toward the cockpit.

"You!" Mort said, pointing a finger squarely at Esper. "Fetch my things. The staff is in plain view, the robe hanging in the closet, my chain of office is under the dirty laundry pile."

"But why can't—"

"Just do it!" Mort snapped. He leapt to he feet and paced the common room, hands outstretched. Esper edged past him and opened the door to his quarters.

She had poked her head inside Mort's quarters once or twice, but never set so much as a foot within. She had, in fact, avoided going inside anyone else's quarters but her own since she'd been aboard the ship. But she had made especially sure to steer clear of the living quarters of Mordecai The Brown. Issues of privacy and personal space aside, there was something unnatural about the air that wafted out the door each time it opened. It was anachronism embodied in a cloister of a bedroom, from the antique wrought iron candleholders to the shelves filled with paper books; it belonged in a museum or a retrovert colony, not aboard a starship.

But there was an urgent need, and Esper had no time to worry that she was stepping into the seventeenth century as she crossed the threshold. There was a musty smell inside, something that the ship's air filtration seemed unable to remedy, but she was otherwise no worse for her entry into Mort's domain. From the rugs thrown across the steel floor to the clutter that hung from every wall, it would have been easy to fool herself into believing she was in an old-Earth cottage from a holovid—if not for the massive window that showed the moon Drei rapidly falling away beneath them.

Esper found the staff first, resting against the headboard of Mort's bed, and she used the butt end of it to shift aside soiled wizard-wear on the floor until a silver chain emerged from the pile of cloth. The metal was pleasantly warm in her hand, reminding her that it was no ordinary substance. Each link was as thick as her little finger, and the pendant that hung from it bore the insignia of the Convocation—a letter 'C' struck through with a lightning bolt. Mort's closet was a jumble of sweatshirts and novelty sweaters from dozens of different worlds, but one leather garment bag stood apart from the rest. Unzipping it, she found a well-tended robe, cleaner and in better repair than anything else in Mort's closet.

Back in the common room, she helped Mort wriggle into the robe and then handed over the staff and chain. The blue atmosphere outside the overhead dome was tinged in red as the *Mobius'* shields ignited the oxygen and forced it out of their path. The fires gave way to the quiet, endless void of the Black Ocean as they achieved orbit. The ship shuddered.

"We're parking," Carl's voice came over the intra-ship comm. "Get us out of real-space before the satellite defenses pulverize us." As if to emphasize his point, the ship shook once more.

Mort pointed to a seat on the couch. "Silent. Still. Understood?"

Esper nodded, keenly aware of the first of Mort's commandments.

With a flourish that sent the voluminous sleeves of his robe fluttering, Mort spread his arms, staff held clutched in one hand. Raising Earth-born old wood over his head, he grabbed hold of it with his other hand as well and slammed the butt end to the floor. The ship convulsed, and Esper couldn't tell whether it was Mort's doing or the work of Drei's defense force. Either way, the Black Ocean's eponymous color soon faded to the now-familiar grey of astral space as Mort chanted. She had heard his spellcasting before, but this time there was an urgency in his voice, something plaintiff and raw that made her curious what sort of argument he and the universe were having. Being magical itself, it was strange that the earring charm she wore couldn't—or wouldn't—translate it.

Esper expected Mort to stop at any moment, but he kept up his chant. He gestured with his hands and shook his staff as if some rival debater threatened to win the day. The flat gray outside the domed glassteel ceiling deepened, not darker but rather acquiring an element of depth that it had previously lacked. Esper dug her fingers into the couch cushions to hold on as vertigo swept over her, but she couldn't bring herself to look away or close her eyes. It seemed an affront to the wonder before her not to witness it. An iridescence swirled in as Mort's chanting grew frantic. Soon the whole sky shifted in swirls and whorls of purple. The purple darkened and reddened as

Mort screamed primordial syllables. Esper spared a glance from the astral miracle outside to see Mort's face dripping sweat. With a final shout and the slamming of his staff once more against the steel floor, the sky settled back into purple and stayed that way.

Mort stood panting, leaning on his staff for support. "That ought to do it."

"So..." Esper said, not quite sure what to say after such a display. "Where are we?"

Mort managed a weary chuckle. "Damned if I know. We're not dead. The rest can wait. I need a nap." Without any further comment he shambled off toward his quarters.

Soon after the door thumped shut, Carl peeked into the room from the cockpit corridor. "What the *hell* was that?"

Esper felt drained. Her fingers were stiffened into claws from gripping the fabric of the couch, and whatever worries had welled within her had been siphoned out by Mort's simple pronouncement that they were still alive. "Well, Mort purpled the universe, but I'm guessing you could see that up front. He almost redded it, which I gather would have been bad, but he managed to convince it to be purple for us instead. If you want a better answer, you're going to have to wait out Mort's nap. How deep did he put us, anyway?"

Tanny walked in behind Carl. "We've got no way to tell. The astral depth sensors work by scanning progressive depths back to real-space to pick up E-M radiation. They can't find real-space from where we are."

"So..." Esper said.

"We could be five minutes from any system in the galaxy," Carl said, "but with no way to navigate."

"Does this happen often?" Bryce Brisson was out of sight down the corridor, but Esper knew his voice by process of elimination.

"No," Esper replied with a sigh. "It's something different every time."

❀ ❀ ❀

Roddy walked into the common room to find the rest of the crew sitting around in an uncomfortable silence, along with their new passenger.

"I know I'm not gonna like the answer," he said, "But what the hell just happened? The engines went into an overload lock and restart, and that's about the best news I've got."

"I'd have called down to tell you," Carl replied, "But the comm's down."

Roddy lifted his palms to the ceiling. "You couldn't have, maybe, *yelled down* or something?"

"Didn't think you'd take this long coming up."

"I'm the mechanic, and the *Mobius* is falling apart around me," Roddy griped. "Either Mort fucked something up, or the planetary defenses got us and this is hell."

"Pretty sure this isn't what hell would be like," Esper replied.

"Although ..." Carl said, taking aim with the holovid remote and pressing several buttons with no response. "Adrift with a blown holo-projector would be a good start."

Roddy frowned. "Gimme that!" He took the remote and ambled over to the holo-projector, pressing buttons all the way. "What the ..." he muttered to himself. Prying open an access panel, he peered inside. One of the circuit cards popped out after a brief wiggle. "*This* shouldn't be possible. This thing's right in the middle of where Mort always stands to send us astral; it's packed with more glyphed obsidian rods than ... well anything I've ever worked on. That's for sure." He shoved the circuit card into Carl's hands.

He took it gingerly, as if it would be hot, but it was just cool, hard plastic. Holding it up to his eye, he squinted at the surface and noticed the striations across the whole length of the card. "What am I looking at?"

"Those ripples," Roddy said, "Those aren't supposed to be there at all. It's like ... I dunno, we went astral faster in some parts of the ship than others. Engines took a bit of roughing up—not as bad as this. But the *Mobius* just got pressed through a toothsoap tube or something."

Carl sighed. "Well, I guess no holovid to watch while we wait for Mort to wake up and get us back to a depth we can—"

"You're not getting it," Roddy said. "There's no more holovid until we buy a new one. Circuit traces are disrupted and cross-connected. The data matrix is scrambled eggs. This thing's nothing but an awkward table now."

"The main computer is still fine," Tanny said. "I mean, we can't compute a heading, but the nav-comp *knows* we can't."

"We're lucky fucks, then," Roddy replied.

"Well," Bryce said. "At least they stopped shooting at us."

Carl chuckled. "They did, at that. Gotta wonder what those trigger-happy bastards were thinking when we dropped off the far end of the astral sensors."

"Yeah," Tanny said dryly, folding her arms. "I feel much better knowing that we crippled our ship to confuse some pisspot lunar militia who wanted you for questioning."

"Better than taking a chance," Carl replied. He turned to Bryce. "Since there's nothing to watch, want to see your quarters?"

The converted conference room echoed their footsteps as Carl and Bryce entered. Aside from a cot and a rickety bedside table, the room was empty. The full-wall window cast everything in a hazy purple hue from the strange astral space outside.

"Cozy," Bryce said deadpan.

"Reminds me of a song," Carl replied.

"Considering the fare you're charging, I was getting a little embarrassed," Bryce said. He unslung the pack from his shoulder and pressed it into Carl's hands. "Now it seems like a fair trade."

Carl grimaced. After all they had just been through, it didn't seem right taking everything Bryce had left. "Sorry," he said. "I just can't—"

"Like hell you can't," Bryce replied. "A deal's a deal."

Curiosity piqued, Carl unbuckled the pack and peeked inside. A smattering of A-tech devices nestled among a change of clothes. He was no expert, but the brands were top-of-the-line: ClanCore, Nano Nano, Fylax, and one in laaku that he recognized by logo alone. "Lemme guess ..."

"Yup," Bryce said. He looked Carl up and down. "Clothes'll probably be a bit loose on you, but they're worth more than the pile of scrap circuits after your wizard's little stunt."

"He means well."

Bryce turned his back and meandered over to the window. "Not my problem, now. All I've got is a ticket to a system of my choosing."

"About that ..."

Bryce whirled, scowling. "You're not stiffing me."

Carl held up his hands. There was a good chance that the blaster in Bryce's holster was at least temporarily out of commission, if not permanently fried. Mort was asleep. Tanny and Mriy were too far to intervene. It was the sort of survival math that ran through Carl's head any time danger presented itself outside a cockpit environment. "'Course not! You just haven't mentioned where you're going."

Bryce nodded to himself and scratched beneath an ear. "Yeah. Guess I haven't. You know the Freeride System?"

"Sure," Carl replied. The official name was Syrbaat, or Syerbat or something tongue-twisting, but hardly anyone called it by that name. Certainly, no one who belonged there would use the scientific nomenclature. "The Poet Fleet's turf. We've been out that way before. Not the nicest neighborhood, but if you wanted to travel in the protection of ARGO's loving chokehold you wouldn't have hired us."

Bryce gave him a puzzled look. "You're not even going to haggle?"

Carl puzzled right back at him. "What do you mean?"

"I paid you with a sack of dead A-tech and my dirty laundry," Bryce replied, prompting Carl to hold the pack away from him. "And then I ask you to take me halfway across ARGO space to a system with black-level security."

"Like you said," Carl replied. "A deal's a deal. Besides, black schmack. Security is fine out there if you play by their rules. It's just not *ARGO* security. Hell, maybe we can find some work out there to pay for repairs."

"So ... you're not even worried about this?" Bryce asked, jerking a thumb at the swirling chaos outside the ship.

"Just looking at it makes me want to vomit," Carl confessed. "But Mort'll get us out of this. Don't worry. Just *whatever* you do, don't wake him up."

Bryce grunted. "Grumpy wizard. Tell me something new."

"Not grumpy," Carl corrected. "Forgetful. Might take him a minute to remember we brought you on with us. Last thing you want is Mort thinking you're an intruder."

"I'll keep that in mind," Bryce said. He flopped down onto the bed with a long-suffering sigh. "Does this bed smell like dog?"

"No," Carl replied. "Of course not."

Kubu sat on Mommy's bed. It was nice enough—the blankets smelled like her. She had left him a bucket of water and a pair of boots to chew on, but there wasn't much else to do in the little room. There was nothing to look at outside the window, just a lot of purple sky. The purple sky had stopped being interesting once Kubu realized there were no birds or animals out in it. It was just a boring purple sky.

Kubu was hungry. He was usually hungry enough to eat, but this was the bad kind of hungry that made him wish that Mommy's boots were just a little easier to chew. The dry slab of meat she had left with him was a faint memory in his tummy, already grumbled up and ready to drop somewhere later—but not in Mommy's room. Mommy had trouble getting her point across most of the time, but she'd managed to make that one clear.

Mommy had been gone too long. There was a chance that she might never come back. A rational part of Kubu's brain told him that was silly, and that Mommy would be back; that kept him from being sad about his temporary abandonment. The less rational part told him that he needed to eat something, even if it wasn't yummy.

Yelling at the door did no good. He'd tried it enough times to know that Mommy couldn't hear him through it. Mommy's ears weren't very good, because he could hear voices on the other side sometimes. He tried to open the door himself, but his paws couldn't work the handle. It was time to take matters into his own jaws.

Mommy didn't keep lots and lots of things in her room. There were her dress-up clothes, and the leash and harness he had to wear when they went outside the ship. There was a big box he couldn't get open, and a few funny-tasting things that were too hard to gnaw on. Kubu nosed around the room, sniffing everywhere he could find for something to eat. Here and there, he pushed aside one of Mommy's strange things or dug behind something to see if anything was hidden there.

He found a bunch of small boxes. They were tucked behind a piece of wall that had just enough room for Kubu to fit a claw into. Mommy ate from a little box just like that every morning. The box was metal, but it cracked open when he bit it and little bits of food fell out with a few shakes. They didn't taste good, but Kubu was hungry, and they were better than nothing—or metal boxes.

It was a lot of work for how little food was in each one, but on the off chance that Mommy might not be back for a long time, Kubu emptied them all. By the time he was finished, if it was possible, he was even *hungrier*. Mommy's little foods were broken. They didn't sate Kubu's hunger; they didn't taste good, and his tummy was starting to gurgle. There weren't a lot of things Kubu had eaten that made his tummy bubble. There was a bucket of bad water in the mean science man's big house that had made him sick. Some spotted mushrooms had made his head funny and his insides wobbly. And one time Kubu had eaten a bunch of little frogs without chewing them first; those felt so bad in his tummy that he puked them back up and didn't even bother eating them again.

This was worse than all of those put together. His head was wobbling, his legs had gone jittery, and the room was getting too hot around him. Kubu was *angry* that Mommy had left him alone. How dare she not give him enough food and make him eat the yucky tiny food in the metal boxes. Kubu's breath came quick and heavy. He bit the mattress from Mommy's bed shook it. It was dry in his mouth though, and Kubu was beginning to notice just how thirsty he was becoming.

With effort, Kubu stood on his hind legs and turned the faucet with a paw. Jamming his face into the sink, he lapped up the water as fast as his tongue would flick. *Mommy, where are you? Kubu isn't feeling good.*

Compared to the homey comfort of the pilot's seat, the co-pilot's side of the *Mobius* felt weird. Tanny hated having Carl there while she flew, and Mriy wasn't much of a conversationalist. The only times he sat in the cockpit were the few occasions when he got to fly. There was a perspective shift that made everything look wrong, like trying to fire a blaster left-handed or sitting on the wrong side of a holovid field.

Of course, the lack of holovid entertainment was the main reason Carl was up front in the first place. The nav computer wasn't much of a pastime, but it beat sitting in a quiet common room with a dead holo-projector.

"This is pointless," Tanny griped. "It's not like anything we plot will be worth a damn once Mort brings us up. The course will change depending on our depth."

Carl rubbed his eyes with his fingers. "I just wanted an idea how long this trip was going to be. If you'd rather just sit here and talk, though, fine."

Tanny cast Carl a narrow glance, then returned her attention to the computer. "If he brings us down to anything around ten astral units, you can figure on a week and a half to get there."

"What about fifteen?" Carl asked.

"Jesus, how deep do you think we *are*?"

"Can't say for certain. All I know is we're in a ..." he reached for a button on the console.

"Not again! Just—"

"*Purple haze, all around* ..." the computer managed before Tanny could squelch the audio playback. Carl giggled.

"You just don't get tired of that joke? How is it that your shitty old music has something for every occasion? We're lost at the deep end of astral space, and some fucker 600 years ago wrote a song, just in case."

"Esper said it got red for a few seconds before Mort settled us in," Carl replied. "If it had stayed red, I didn't have a song for that."

Tanny snorted. "You'd have forced something to fit."

"Hey, how often do you find yourself in a ..."

This time, Tanny caught Carl by the wrist as he reached for the audio controls.

"Purple haze?" Carl sang the line himself.

"I wish Mort had fried the song library," Tanny muttered.

"Hey, at least *you* had your holovids stored in the ship's computer. Me and Roddy lost everything."

"What a shame," Tanny deadpanned.

"Hey, I'm just trying to keep a rosy outlook here, but ..." Purple haze, the ship supplied, "is actually freaking me out a little. Is that what you wanted to hear? Mort can't wake up too soon to fix this, far as I'm concerned."

"You warned the fare?"

"Yeah, Bryce got the standard warning. I don't think he'd dare go near Mort at this point, let alone startle him awake."

Sybil and the Sunspots blared a tinny melody from the built-in speakers on Esper's datapad. She kept the volume low so that no one would hear through the walls with the eerie quiet that lingered throughout the ship. It had been years since she'd listened to the group, one of her favorites growing up. It seemed naive and immature now, but when she was twelve it had been profound. Still, it was a comfort, something familiar like the deep black that usually filled the window of her quarters. Esper mouthed along with the words, not quite daring to ask her questionable singing voice to follow the melody out loud.

> *Every sky is a blue sky,*
> *If you raise yourself above the clouds,*
> *If you want your soul to fly,*
> *Just sing and raise your voice up loud.*

Esper swayed as she lip-synced, remembering the concert her friend Novembra's mother had taken them to on Phobos. It had been her first trip off Mars, and she could still remember feeling queasy in the unfamiliar gravity until the music started. Sybil and the Sunspots had been on the downside of their popularity by then, but it hadn't mattered; the whole day had been magical, one new experience after another. The little datapad sitting in Esper's lap was struggling to compete with those fond memories, failing to wash away the constant reminder outside her window that all was decidedly not right in the universe just then.

The purple radiance in the deepest reaches of astral space was hypnotic. As much as she tried to push it from her mind, she found herself staring into it once more, as if some great mystery would unfold before her eyes and make sense of the cosmos. There was motion within the radiance, not objects trapped within the deep astral but a movement of the colors themselves. Light and dark hues swirled like oil droplets in water, never mixing to form a uniform shade of violet. Esper's childhood perception tests had placed her within half a standard deviation from the mean on color identification— she had no artist's eye for colors. But staring into the astral depths, she began to note an overall brightening, and perhaps a hint of too much red creeping in.

Her stomach churned as she watched, wondering if she was the only one paying attention to the ship's plight as it teetered on the edge of astral space so deep they might never return. She moved to stand, to run and shout throughout the ship that they were dropping deeper, but forced herself to sit. It was just her imagination, she convinced herself. Mort went to take a well-deserved rest, and he never would have left them in such peril.

But what if he didn't realize?

Esper clasped her hands in her lap, her grip growing ever more desperate as she watched out the window. Doing nothing might get them all killed. She had to go wake Mort. He could be angry with her all he liked, but the time for peaceful napping was over, wizard or not.

She tore open the door to her quarters and rushed across the empty common room to Mort's. It was doubly odd: once for the emptiness and quiet instead of the every-present holovids, twice for the purple illumination from the domed ceiling. She didn't bother knocking, just opened the door and peeked inside. Mort snored softly, sleeping fully dressed atop his blankets. He had the look of a vagrant with his stained, worn clothes and unshaven face, mouth hanging agape. He stirred at the opening of the door, but did not wake.

"Mort?" Esper whispered, seeking a gentle waking. "Mort ..." she tried once more, in a normal tone of voice. The snoring carried on uninterrupted. With a glance behind her for gossiping eyes, she slipped into the room and closed the door behind her. Tiptoeing across the room for reasons she would struggle to explain if asked, she crept to Mort's bedside. "Mort," she crooned, in her best imitation of her mother's summonses from dreamland when she was a girl. "Time to—"

Mort's hand shot up and caught her by the upper arm. "Who are you? What ... how did you get in here?"

Esper's whole body tensed. "It's me, Esper," she replied. "I came in by—"

"You can't fool me," Mort said, sitting up but not relinquishing his grip. His fingers dug into Esper's bicep and triceps, and she gritted her teeth. She was only thankful he didn't have Tanny's strength or Mriy's claws. "Esper is in the reliquary. I left her there not ten minutes ago. Now speak, or I'll tear the secrets from your mind." With his free hand, Mort took hold of Esper's chin and tried to look into her eyes, but she averted her gaze in time.

With a leverage technique she had learned from Tanny, Esper wrenched herself free of Mort's grasp. "It *is* me," she insisted. "You were dreaming. This is the *Mobius*. We need your help. We're slipping deeper into the astral plane."

"*Mobius* ..." Mort repeated, then nodded slowly. He looked around the room for the first time since waking. "Of course it is ..." He cleared his throat and blinked several times. "Sorry about that. Didn't anyone mention never to wake me when—"

Esper pointed out the window. "There's no time."

Mort followed her finger's indication and looked out upon the purple void. After a moment's inspection, he asked, "How can you tell?"

"Can't you see it? The color is changing?"

Mort gave a twitch of a shrug and a tilt of his head. "Not really, no."

"It's getting darker and redder," Esper said, shaking her pointing finger at the purple. "I'd tell you just to keep watching, but if we *are* drifting, that seems like a bad idea."

"Well, your supposition would be correct if the color were changing," Mort said. "I just don't see it, though."

Esper's eyes went wide. "No! You have to believe me."

Mort shrank back and furrowed his brow. "What?" he asked. "I never said I didn't believe you. Best to bring us back up, before it gets worse. Half a nap's better than none."

Esper folded her hands together and closed her eyes. As she began a silent prayer of thanks, a gentle tug separated her hands. "Don't go giving Him the credit. It's my help you asked for. If you wanted a miracle, you should have asked for one. But you wanted magic, so it's me you came to. If you want to be useful, just tell Him to keep out of the way and let me do my job." As Mort stepped around Esper on his way to the door, he paused and leaned close. "And if I fuck this up, *then* you can pray for help."

When Esper and Mort entered the common room, they discovered that they weren't the only ones there. Carl and Tanny stood with backs turned, staring at the door to Tanny's quarters. A thump issued from the door, and the sound of a muffled growl.

"What's going on?" Esper asked.

Carl twisted around, frowning at the open door to Mort's quarters and the two of them standing just outside it. "Were you two just—? Never mind. Something's wrong with Kubu. He's flipping out in there."

"It's OK, Kubu," Tanny called through the door. "Just ... calm down, and I'll open the door and let you out." She looked over her shoulder. "You guys might want to keep back, just in case."

"If he's gone all zoological, I can—"

"No!" Tanny and Carl shouted in unison, then exchanged a frowning glance.

"Sorry, Mort," Carl replied. "*Mobius* is just a little fragile right now. You zorched the holovid and gave the engines the hiccups. Roddy's pulling his fur out down in the engine room as it is. Aside from bringing us up to a traversable depth, I think you might want to ease off the magic for a while."

"No holovid?" Mort asked.

Carl shook his head.

Mort folded his arms and let out a disgusted sigh. "Blast and be bothered. Was the fridge affected?"

"Beer's fine," Carl confirmed.

"Well, there's that at least."

There was a howl from inside Tanny's quarters. "If you ladies wouldn't mind, get behind cover."

Carl scurried over to join Mort and Esper behind the couch. "Were you two just ... alone?" he asked as he hunkered down.

"Limit your filthy mind to its own affairs," Mort warned. "Esper noticed we're still drifting deeper and came to find me."

"What do you mean, we're—"

Carl's question was cut short by an ear-splitting howl as Tanny opened the door. Kubu bounded from Tanny's quarters like a canine avalanche, bowling Tanny over as if she were a child. She fell back, struck her head on the steel floor, and lay still. Kubu ignored her and headed straight for the refrigerator. "Hungry, hungry, hungry, hungry," he said. Jaws like a hydraulic clamp latched onto the door handle and yanked the fridge open before the handle broke loose and Kubu spat it onto the floor.

Kubu's single-minded assault targeted foodstuffs indiscriminately. He gobbled down leftover meals from the food processor and a half wheel of cheese that had gone so moldy that no one wanted to touch it. Carl let out a quiet yelp as Kubu bit into can after can of beer, sucking out the fizzing spray of liquid before chewing and swallowing the cans themselves.

Esper moved to approach the canine, but Carl put a hand on her shoulder. "He's hurting himself," Esper said. "Look, his gums are bleeding from the cans."

"What do you think those teeth would do to *you?*" Carl asked.

The door to Mriy's quarters opened, and the azrin emerged, yawning and rubbing an eye with the back of one paw. "What's all the—" She looked toward Kubu.

"Watch out!" Carl shouted across the room. Kubu turned from the fridge and looked right at him. The eyes were vacant, bloodshot, and glassy. A froth of saliva, beer, and blood dripped from the corners of his mouth and from the tip of his lolling tongue. His chest heaved for breath, but his head remained motionless, fixed on the shouted challenge. A bass growl rumbled in Kubu's throat.

The languorous vestiges of slumber evaporated from Mriy as she sprang forward. Before Kubu could leap at Carl, she had her arms around his neck. Kubu thrashed in her grasp, trying to twist loose, but Mriy bore him to the floor under her weight. As the canine struggled to regain his feet, Mriy used her elbows to knock his legs out from under him.

In the momentary reprieve, Esper rushed to Tanny's side. Putting a finger to her throat, Esper felt a pulse. A small puddle of blood was forming beneath Tanny's head. Esper opened one of Tanny's eyelids with her thumb, and found wide pupils and no sign of reflexive response. Esper was no doctor—she hadn't even taken an emergency aid class. All she had to rely on were the scenes from the holovids she had seen countless times. Tanny either had a concussion, a brain aneurysm, or had seen a nebula demon—and they weren't in any sort of nebula, plus she had seen Kubu knock Tanny to the ground. Odds were, she would recover in time, possibly with amnesia or a weird speech condition. In any event, she had to do something.

Esper placed her hands on either side of Tanny's face, putting Mriy's struggles with Kubu from her mind. The skin was already cool to the touch; there was no time to waste. Her lips moved, but she gave no voice to the little rhyme she and her friends had learned to work the spell of healing. *"Cuts close, bruises fade; three weeks healing done today; bones knit, pains ease; cleanse the body of disease."* She repeated it over and over, and felt Tanny's skin warm feverishly beneath her palms.

Tanny sat up suddenly with a gasp, clutching her stomach. She grunted in pain. "What did you do to me, Esper?"

Esper let out a sigh of relief. "Good, no amnesia. Kubu knocked you out cold. Your head was bleeding, and you weren't waking up."

"But my stomach is on fire," Tanny replied with a grimace. "And what's Mriy doing to Kubu?" She tried to stand, lurching for the wrestling match by the refrigerator, but doubled over instead.

"You need food," Esper replied. "The healing takes a lot out of you."

"And here I thought Carl ... was being a baby about the hunger pangs ... that time you healed him."

"Is it safe to get in there?" Esper called across to Mriy.

"I can hold him away from the food long enough for you to get in," Mriy answered. For all Kubu's compact strength and frenzied struggles, Mriy was nearly twice his mass. She kept him pinned to the floor as he tried to squirm loose and reach the open fridge and what little remained untouched within.

Esper hurried past the struggling pair, tiptoeing around a splatter of ketchup from a ruptured bottle and a small lake of spilled beer. The shelves inside the fridge were in shambles, and not much was left inside that was either edible or potable. Esper grabbed whatever she could lay hands on and returned to Tanny.

"Here," she said, dumping the armload beside Tanny and beginning an inventory. She found the first filling-looking thing in the pile and pressed an eggplant casserole E-Z-Meal into Tanny's hands.

"Who the hell bought this?" Tanny asked accusingly as she tore open the package.

"That would be me," Esper replied. "It was our first stop after I joined the crew. I ... I hadn't remembered how good bacon cheeseburgers were, and I just never got around to—"

"Fine," Tanny replied. "Whatever ..." she muttered as she shoveled the self-warming pasta into her mouth with her fingers. Her head lifted at a canine yelp and subsequent whine. "Mriy, get off Kubu! What do you think you're doing?" At least, that was what Esper imagined she said through a mouthful of eggplant, cheese, and pasta.

"He fights!" Mriy replied. "You were already defeated when I came out."

Tanny cast a suspicious eye into her quarters and the shambles inside. Esper pressed a bottle of peach liquor into her hands and Tanny popped the top with her thumb and sucked half of it down in a few continuous chugs. All the while, she drifted cautiously into the wreckage left in her room. "Shit," she said, wiping her mouth on the sleeve of her jacket. "Esper, where'd the med kit from the conference room end up?"

"It's down in the—"

"Go grab it. Quick. We need to tranq him."

Esper nodded and edged past Mriy and Kubu, still struggling on the floor. Mriy had the canine under control, but that didn't stop his constant efforts to get free. He seemed wild, too far past rational thought even to put words to his frustrations any longer. He snapped at Esper's ankle as she came near, but Mriy got a paw under his jaw and held it shut.

"Should we do anything?" Mort whispered from the corner.

"Hell no," Carl replied in kind, peering over the arm of the couch. "They've got it under control. Plus it's like a full-room holo-projector. Best thing I've watched all day."

Esper knocked on the door of the guest quarters, using the butt of her fist. It was a sturdy door, and any other knock would be either too quiet, or hurt her hand. The door's thickness, and perhaps some trick of its design as a conference room door, prevented her hearing the telltale noises of someone coming to answer.

"Is it safe to come out?" Bryce asked as he opened the door a crack.

"All clear," Esper confirmed, trying to sound as perky as possible. No one else seemed inclined to look after their paying customer's happiness, so it had fallen to her.

The door opened all the way, and Bryce slumped against the opening. "I don't know what the deal is with you people, but astral space just was purple for the last three hours, and I thought I heard a wild animal out there."

Esper pursed her lips and frowned. "I'm not sure how much I can do about that. We might have a spare rug or blanket around somewhere that we can use as additional soundproofing. I'll see what I can—"

"Was there?"

"Was there what?"

"A wild animal."

Esper gave a nervous chuckle. "No, Kubu's domesticated ... sort of. I mean, we don't know what he is, exactly, but he is *very* dog-like. And usually he's pretty friendly, but we cooped him up too long while you were settling in, and he got rowdy." It wasn't the whole story, Esper knew, but it was as much as Tanny had been willing to share on short notice.

Bryce nodded along like someone who was hearing information but failing to absorb it. "Rowdy ..."

Esper nodded exuberantly. "All taken care of. Poor little guy's sleeping it off—erm, behind a locked door."

Bryce swallowed and licked dry lips. "You guys got any food aboard? I was getting a bit between meals when we tucked our tails back on Drei."

It was a subject that was guaranteed to come up sooner or later, but Esper had been hoping it would have leaned toward the later end—when someone else might be around to answer.

"Sort of. That is ... I mean ... don't worry, none of us are going to starve or anything like that."

"What's that supposed to mean? Something happen to your supplies?"

"Kubu ... I mean. Yes. But don't worry."

"Listen," Bryce said. "You've got food or you don't. What's to eat around here?"

"We've got sandwich bread we pried out of the food processor along with a dozen centimeters of salami, some salsa dip, and a jar of huckleberry jam."

"That's it?" Bryce asked with a note of alarm in his voice.

"It's a good-sized jar," Esper assured him. "And don't worry, we're due planetside in eighteen hours or so. We'll get some real food there."

"Where we stopping off?"

"Freeride," Esper replied.

"No, I mean on the way? Freeride's weeks from here, even if this thing's flying below military courier depths."

"No, just about eighteen hours," Esper said. "I think if you look out that window some more, you'll see that the gray's still got a tinge of purple in it. So just relax, grab yourself a jam sandwich, and we'll have you to Freeride in no time."

✳ ✳ ✳

Bryce emerged from his rented quarters like a rehabilitated animal being returned to the wild. He looked poised to bolt at any moment for the relative safety of his room. The veneer of cocksure swagger he'd displayed on Drei had rubbed off to reveal a timid tech jockey underneath.

"Come on and join us," Carl offered, beckoning him over the heads of Mort and Roddy. "Pull up a chair. The cards are analog, so they're still working fine. We're playing for dibs on the last bottle of anything drinkable that isn't water." Carl cast a sidelong glance to Roddy, who he knew kept an emergency supply of Earth's Preferred under his bed, but didn't see the point in mentioning that in front of Bryce.

They were gathered at the kitchen table in the common room, next to the refrigerator with its door held shut by mechanics' tape. At the center of the table was the last bottle of Esper's peach liquor. She had donated it to the cause of intra-ship harmony, and declined to play for it, along with Tanny who had drunk the second-to-last bottle already. Mriy was back in her quarters, exhausted after her prolonged struggle with Kubu.

"What are you playing?" Bryce asked, pulling out a chair and settling in beside Mort.

Carl pushed a pile of loose hardware in Bryce's direction. "Poker. Five card stud. Old school as hell, to humor Mort. You know it?"

"Yeah," Bryce mumbled, looking down at the assorted steel hardware in front of him. "What's all this for?"

"Since we're playing for the booze, we're using those instead of hard-coin. Nuts are fives; washers are ones. Those broken rivet heads are twenty-five apiece."

"Um, sure," Bryce replied. "The girl mentioned something about sandwiches."

Roddy reached back for a plate stacked with square-cut bread designed to feed into the loader of a food-processor. "Knock yourself out. Jam, salami, and mustard are in the freezer. I turned the reducer down to act as a fridge."

Bryce sat out the first two hands as he made himself a sad little meal. Carl didn't mention that the salami was three months past expiration, and that Roddy had hacked the food processor to accept later and later dates to keep it from auto-dumping it.

"Fancy grub," Bryce muttered through a mouthful of dry bread and spoiled salami as he sat down. "Listen, Carl, you and me gotta talk. Is it true we're less than a day out of Freeride?"

"It's all right there in the computers," Carl replied. "Shit, if we could make contact with anyone official, we'd probably be up for some sort of record. Fella could get used to crossing the galaxy at these speeds."

"Don't go getting used to it," Mort interjected. "You're only smug about it because you can't wrap your science-filled head with just how close we all came to oblivion."

"How close *did* we come?" Bryce asked.

Mort raised one eyebrow and squinted at Bryce with the other eye. "I'll tell you how close, tech-boy. We came within the length of a dragon's whisker, the breadth of a silkworm's sigh. There was time, perhaps, for one syllable of the Cladis Grimoire to pass a fool's lips before creation itself snuffed us like a birthday candle."

"Oh," Bryce said.

"Ante up," Roddy said, tossing in two washers.

Bryce tossed two of his own into the middle of the table and cleared his throat. "So anyway ... thought I'd have more time in transit, but we need to talk."

"Can you talk and play at the same time?" Carl asked. Bryce nodded. "Then shoot."

Roddy flicked cards around the table with casual precision. Aside from a peek at his facedown cards, Carl didn't bother moving his from where they came to a halt. Mort tidied his cards manually, pointedly not using his magic. Bryce packed his tight and lined them up like inventory on a store shelf.

Secretive. Organized. Obsessive. Carl filed the traits away in case they ever became useful.

"Well, I don't have a job lined up when I get there," Bryce began.

Roddy let out a quick burst of shrieking simian laughter. "Boy, you're pumpin' from a dry well here."

Bryce waved a hand. "No, nothing like that. I've got a line on a job, see? It's just I could use a reference. You know, some sort of good word to get a foot in the door."

"Sure, I guess," Carl replied with a shrug. "You didn't get a chance to show off with the defenses at Drei, but if that had worked... *Man* would that have been something to see. All those defense cannons and ships with their heads spinning, chasing after phantom ships. If you're half as good as you can promise people in desperate need without actually delivering jack shit, then you'd be a credit to anyone looking for one of whatever you actually are."

"He's a doorstop salesman, right?" Roddy asked. "Had a whole pack filled with samples."

"Can it, banana-brain," Bryce snapped, jabbing a finger in the laaku's direction. "Ain't my fault the A-tech I bartered for this hay-ride got wizard-twisted. I'm not asking for charity. I'll make it worth your while."

"How much you thinking?" Carl asked. It was about time to try pinning Bryce to a sum of terras expressed as an actual number, with digits and everything, rather than vague promises and mystery gear.

"Well, I've got ten grand in digital terras, but I might be able to do better in barter," Bryce said.

"In case you hadn't noticed," Roddy said, "We might be in need of repairs. Repairs in a place like Freeride won't come cheap, and they prefer hard-coin terras. Digital might get us somewhere, but chickens, or booze, or whatever shit you're hoping to trade us better convert into a payment to a starship-grade garage."

"There is that," Carl agreed.

"What if I got your criminal records expunged?"

Carl looked to Roddy, then to Mort. Mort and Roddy exchanged a glance of their own. The same skepticism was on every face. "How exactly you planning to pull that shit off?" Carl asked.

"Same way techsters have been beating encryption for centuries: human weaknesses in the system," Bryce said. "All the best have heartbeat ins at anyplace they want to breach. Some careless, some on the take, mostly just idiots who don't even know they're getting used. It's not all strings of zeroes through fifteens in a computer core. Those are just the accessories. It's the people who service and maintain the systems—they're the real weakness."

"So, who've you got who can alter ARGO law enforcement records galaxy-wide?" Carl asked, discarding a bum hand as the bet came his way.

"That's my value: I know and you don't. I send the right message *from* the right guy *to* the right guy, and some terminal data-entry drone processes the request."

"Just like that? Won't that look a little suspicious?"

"Please ... he'll see your record update right in between entering a court date for an assault trial and authorizing a petty cash expenditure to pay off an informant. You're nothing special; just another box to check off before he can go grab lunch."

"Yeah, smart guy?" Roddy asked. "If you can do all that, why do *you* still have a record?"

"The banana-brain's got you on that one," Mort said.

Bryce shrugged. "I've done my time. Sure, I could wipe it out, but what good's that do me? Guy that's been in, you know he's made of something tougher than some pansy who might piss himself if he ever got wind of a little heat. People I'd want to work for would appreciate that."

"What kind of people you talking?" Carl asked.

"Janice Rucker," Bryce said.

There was a long silence. The card game stood still. "So... lemme guess. It's not a coincidence you tracked us down for transport?" Carl asked. "You know who Tanny is."

"Tania Louise Rucker, daughter of Donald and Sue-Ellen Rucker," Bryce replied. "It's sort of my business, figuring out who knows who. Nothing personal. I'd lump you in under 'on the take' for this job. You're no patsy."

"I say we airlock this weasel," Roddy said.

Bryce knocked his chair over as he leapt to his feet and backed away. "Woah! Hear me out!"

"Go on," Carl said with a smirk. "Roddy's just a mean sober; don't mind him."

"We land. I find a terminal, work my mojo, and your records get cleared. You confirm I done my bit, and that's my resume for Janice Rucker."

Carl scratched at the back of his neck. "What's Janny doing out that far? Don likes keeping business close to Mars." It was annoying to have to find out family news from a stranger. Even if Carl was legally divorced from the family, there was no legal force strong enough to entirely remove him from The Family.

"She's branching out, with Don Rucker's blessing," Bryce said. "I haven't been able to sniff out the terms, but she's on her own in exchange for a kickback."

Carl turned to Mort. "See what I have to put up with? If Tanny would talk to her father, we wouldn't have to learn this shit secondhand. We could've hit Janny up for work."

"Which one was she, again?" Roddy asked. "I have trouble keeping Tanny's cousins straight."

"At the wedding, she was the one with the finger-bone earrings," Mort said. "And the five-terra amulet of Kali."

Roddy shuddered. "Ugh. That one's bad news."

"Most of Tanny's family is bad news, if they don't like you," Carl said. "But Janice isn't half as tough as she tries to look."

"That's still twice as scary as I'd want to turn my back on," Roddy said.

Bryce returned to his seat and tossed in a small bet, though the game was quickly becoming an afterthought. "See why I want someone to smooth my intro?"

"Makes sense," Carl admitted.

"So, think Tanny will do it?" Bryce asked. "I mean, even if she's on the outs with her father, you're her captain, and—"

Roddy burst out laughing, and Mort snickered. "Yeah, as if Carl could *order* her to do anything," Roddy said.

"Not to mention, Janny and Tanny don't exactly get along," Carl said. "Nicknames sounded too much alike. Janny's older, but Tanny's Don's daughter, so she was always on a bit of a pedestal. No, it's *me* you want making the introduction, not Tanny."

"You're smooth with Janny?" Bryce asked.

"You're the people researcher," Carl replied. "Janice Rucker seeing anyone?"

Bryce's brow knit for a moment, then he shook his head.

"Then I can be as smooth as I need to," Carl said, tipping back his chair with a smug grin.

"So how do we plot a course change, if we needed to?" Esper asked from the co-pilot's seat. She was sitting with her hands folded in her lap, pointedly not touching anything. The jacket, the coveralls, her hair in a tight bun at the back of her head; everything was just as Tanny had instructed her for getting actual work done aboard ship.

"You don't have to pretend to be interested in this stuff," Tanny replied. "It's sweet that you're worried, but I'm fine now. Thanks." There wasn't even a lingering pain from the blow to her head when Kubu had trampled her. The dumb brute was sleeping off his triple-dose of tranquilizer in her quarters, which had the added bonus of hiding the evidence of what he'd eaten. How could Tanny explain to Esper that the concussion was the least of her troubles.

Tanny's stomach churned, not quite satisfied with the "meal" Esper had scrounged, and even less happy with the alcohol that had washed it down. But those were mere side-effects. The trouble was that Esper's magic had sped her metabolism. She wouldn't know until symptoms started manifesting, but she had burned either hours or days out of her drug regimen, and Kubu had consumed all her recent supplies. The dog-like creature had a digestive tract that a vulture would envy. Had anyone told her a seventy-kilo animal had eaten a two month supply of marine biochemicals, she'd write the creature off as a corpse. Kubu's reaction to the drugs aside, he didn't seem in imminent danger of death.

"I know," Esper replied with a faint smile. It was a trick Carl used. Just agree to shut someone up, and keep on acting like neither of you said anything. "Could I try plotting a heading, and just not confirm?" She reached a finger toward the nav computer.

Tanny batted the hand away, already noticing that her own hand was jittery. "Leave it alone! At this speed, I don't want to touch anything." For at least the hundredth time, she glanced at the astral depth gauge. It read 30.88, with the analogue needle over the digital display pegged at maximum. Before she met Mort, Tanny had figured those gauges only went to up to ten to make ships seem faster than they really were.

"You don't look so good."

"Don't you start that with me," Tanny snapped. Esper had that patronizing look in her eye—pity and sympathy, mixed with a bit of holier-than-thou, I-told-you-so crap.

"Start what?"

"Being a priestess at me."

Esper slumped back in her chair with a sigh. "I don't think I could if I wanted to. I mean, look at me." She gave a two-handed gesture up and down herself. "Who'd come to *me* looking for spiritual solace? I look like an outlaw spacer, because that's what I am, now."

"Worse things to be," Tanny muttered. "But you still act like a priestess, sometimes. You've got a vibe."

"Do I?" Esper asked. "Do I really?" She fished at her collar and drew a chain out from under her shirt. Dangling from the end was a stone in a silver setting; it was bone white except for a bit of pink toward the bottom. "Do you know what this is?"

Tanny shrugged. "A necklace. What, did you steal it from the One Church or something?"

"No, it was a gift from my mother for my twelfth birthday. It's magic."

"What's it do?"

Esper regarded the pendant a moment before answering. "It gets darker toward the end of the month. Swoosh it around in water, and it goes white again, and the water turns red.

How'd my mother put it... ? 'Keeps away cramps and boy problems.'"

"Sounds handy."

Esper gave a delicate snort. "Handy... yeah. I gave it a workout, that's for sure. I should have given it up when I joined the priesthood, but I couldn't part with it. Just a little inconvenience now and then, but I'd gotten so used to it that I was scared what it might be like quitting. I was supposed to be putting my faith in the Lord, setting an example. I mean, I didn't totally hide it, and I had to swear it was for the side benefits and not because I intended to break any vows, but sometimes it felt like an anchor around my neck."

"So?"

"Sound familiar?"

Tanny glared at Esper. What was she getting at? The imbalance of biochemicals in her system was making it hard to concentrate. She had a constant ringing in her ears, and her eyes kept losing focus. There were few enough times when she was in the mood for riddles and innuendo, and this was certainly not among them.

"Kubu didn't get sick eating cosmetics or foot cream," Esper said when it became clear Tanny had no ready reply. "I must have burned something out of your system when I healed that bump you got on the head."

"That fucking bastard," Tanny muttered. Esper had probably confronted Carl and he must have told her. "It's none of your business, and I don't like you going behind my back." Esper flinched back, and that was when Tanny realized she was not only shouting, but leaning toward the co-pilot's chair. She settled back into the pilot's seat and took a calming breath.

"It wasn't Carl," Esper said. "You're coming down off something. You all act like I was born and raised in a convent, but my parents were broke when I was young. We lived in Neo-Rotterdam, and not even the OK part. I saw burn-outs, vapes, glass-eyes, 'roid-mutants, tweakers, and schizoids. The school shuttle pilot had a stim addiction, but no one else would take the job, so they kept him on."

"So that's what you see? A tweaker on a crash?" Fuck Esper. Even when she was trying to act like she grew up tough, she came across like a ... well, like a priestess.

"Everyone's heard about the stuff they give marines. It doesn't take a xenogeneticist to figure out you kept taking it. You can pass it off as lingering effects of the stuff you took while you were in, making you stronger and tougher than everyone. But if you're reacting like *this* to metabolic healing, and sweet, dopey Kubu turned into Cerberus all of a sudden. Come on, I'm not an idiot."

Tanny swallowed. "No, I guess you're not." She let her head loll back against the headrest and closed her eyes.

"You don't have to show me how to navigate if you don't want to," Esper said. "But I'll stay right here, in case you need me."

❀ ❀ ❀

"Bring us to a halt at the edge of the system," Carl said, resting a hand on the back of the pilot's chair. His stomach was undecided between gnawing hunger and wanting to eject the huckleberry and salami sandwich that was the only thing he'd eaten in the past eighteen hours.

Tanny turned and looked up with a question in her eyes. For a split-second, Carl thought it might stay there, but he was disappointed yet again. "What for? It'll take days to cross the system in real-space." There was an edge in her voice, and Carl knew he was walking across springtime ice on a sunny day.

Whatever she was feeling from the lack of her stash, Tanny was in a bad way—pale and glistening with sweat on her brow even in the cool 16°C cockpit.

"Yeah, we could blow by them and they'd never see us," Carl agreed. "But this is the Poet Fleet's turf, and I want to play nice. We'll hail a patrol ship and say 'hi.' They've got intra-system astral gates we can use after that."

"Mort'll be pissed."

"Mort's a big boy," Carl said. "Besides, everyone'll be fine once we get the holo-projector replaced."

Tanny snorted. "Just like that, huh? With what money?"

Carl took a casual step back and out of Tanny's reach. Her attention was back on the ship's controls, so he didn't try to hide his grin. "I figure Janice can spot us."

"Janice ...? Janice who?" Tanny's voice held a note of slow menace.

"Janice Rucker," Carl said. "You know, Jay and Carly's oldest. Seriously, I keep better track of your family than you do. Maybe I can make you a chart or—"

"What's Janice doing out here?"

"Hiring Bryce, hopefully."

"What?"

"Bryce wants a job working for her," Carl said. He shrugged even though Tanny wasn't looking his way. He explained Bryce's plan, and rehashed Mort and Roddy's interrogation of their passenger and his responses. He skipped the part where he implied he might seduce her cousin, but otherwise left nothing out.

"I don't like it," Tanny declared at the end of Carl's story. "Seems too polished. How's this penny-ante data hustler know so much? And if he did, why's he pulling out the overdrive to work for *Janice* of all people? You'd think anyone with three working brain cells would be trying to get *off* her crew, not on it."

"I don't think she's working a crew anymore," Carl replied. "Your dad doesn't like things getting too far out of his sight. This is her own gig, being her own boss."

"You think that's going to make her cupcakes and taffy to work for? That hulking she-beast's probably going to rip people's hearts out with her bare hands when they piss her off."

"Probably good money in it, though," Carl said, stuffing his hands in his pockets.

"Don't you even..." Tanny said. "Didn't you hear a word I said?"

Tanny slowed the ship to a stop. The *Mobius* was at the outer limits of the Freeride System. They were too deep in the astral to pick up anything on sensors—far too deep—but the concealment worked both ways. Nothing should have been traveling this far down; Mort had described the *Mobius* as an elephant walking a tightrope, but Carl figured *anyone* would be able to see that. Mort had tried changing to a non elephant-centric metaphor, but Carl had admitted that he really didn't care, so long as Mort didn't get them stuck in a purple haze again.

"Janny isn't a—"

"Janice," Tanny insisted.

"—isn't a problem at the moment. We've still got to deal with the pirates." Carl keyed the intra-ship comm. "OK, Mort. Set us back in real-space, nice and gentle."

A shout echoed through the corridor from the common room. "Don't tell me my business!"

Carl double-checked to make sure the comm was off. "Geez, who'd have thought the fridge was the key to everyone's mood on this ship," he said to Tanny. Then he caught a glimpse of the bloodshot glare she was giving him. "Present company excluded, of course. Don't worry. Recitol might be tough to find out here, but you can bet the rest is for sale."

"You'd like that, wouldn't you?" Tanny asked with venom.

He shouldn't have mentioned the Recitol. He knew it even as he'd said it. Those pills had been at the center of more arguments between them than any subject except for who should fly the ship. "Just being realistic. Farther you get from Sol, the scarcer it gets."

The gray of astral space darkened into the familiar Black Ocean. Stars perked up against the backdrop of the void, and a tiny speck of yellow light was the Freeride System's sun, Syrbaat—or Syerbat, whichever. Carl could never keep it straight which was a star system and which a cheap brand of recreational land-cruisers. The cosmos was not the only thing to be seen; Tanny had dropped them out at an unofficial checkpoint, a place in-the-know spacers could pay their respects to the Poet Fleet and her commander before venturing into the core of the system. A small fuel depot, a pirate-owned astral gate, and a lone patrol ship waited for them. Just by stopping there, the *Mobius* had shown that they weren't rubes blundering in unawares.

"Weapons lock!" Tanny shouted.

"Shields!" Carl snapped, but Tanny was already lunging for the shield controls.

"*Vessel* Mobius, *power down and prepare for scan*," a voice ordered over the comm.

Carl reached down and hit the button to reply. "Hey there, this is Carl Ramsey, captain of the *Mobius*. No problemo. Powering down. Just... don't shoot us, OK?" Some hasty gesturing ensued, and Tanny shut down the ship's engines and shield generator. Their weapons were already offline, and no one meant life support when they told you to shut everything down. It was just one of those quirks of ship-to-ship communication.

"This is Commander Anabel Sanders of the We Are Pariahs Because We Speak Unpleasant Truths. *How were you able to evade our astral sensors?"*

"Shoot, I'd have to know a lot more about astral sensors to answer that," Carl replied. "We're a bit non-standard in the star-drive department though, so that might explain things. Didn't mean to spook you. I mean, we stopped at your checkpoint and all."

"Yes, you did. What is your destination?"

"Third planet. I forget the local name," Carl replied.

"Sybaat III is called Carousel," Commander Anabel replied. *"Your business there?"*

"Passenger drop off."

"Length of stay?"

"Until we find a job that pays us to go somewhere else."

"Who can vouch for your ship?"

"Shit," Carl said. "I've been here before. Doesn't that count?"

"New security measures. Your ship will be limited to high-security docking if you don't have a sponsor."

"Janice Rucker," Carl replied. Tanny whirled in her seat before he could wipe the grin from his face.

"What philosophers do you follow?"

"Pardon?"

"For example, I follow the tenets of Bushido, and the writings of Nietzsche. Whose philosophies guide you?"

Carl scratched his head. "I don't get that one often, I gotta say. I guess Miller and Stills. I'm a complicated guy, though.

I could list off a few dozen, mood by mood. Is there a wrong answer to this?"

"*Not as such. I just like knowing whom I'm allowing through. I'm not familiar with either a Miller or Stills though.*"

"That's a shame," Carl said. "I can transmit copies of their seminal works."

There was a brief silence on the comm. "You just had to do that," Tanny whispered, as if the ship would transmit without an open comm if she spoke in a normal voice.

"*Very well, Mobius, proceed to the gate. Refrain from using any onboard star-drive systems, regulation or otherwise. I look forward to perusing the works of your philosophers.*"

"See?"

"They're as fucked up as you are," Tanny muttered as she powered up the engines and set a course for the Poet Fleet's astral gate.

The trip through the Poet Fleet's astral gate was uneventful. It was set to 1.5 astral depth, just to keep it separate from the traffic of ships operating under their own star-drives. In the whole two-hour slog through the Freeride System, they only passed two other vessels, one a Saddlebag-class trader broadcasting no ID, the other an interdictor like the *We Are Pariahs Because We Speak Unpleasant Truths*. Its name was *There Is No Soap to Cleanse the Soul,* and was probably set to relieve the *We Are Pariahs Because We Speak Unpleasant Truths* on gate-guard duty. Carl tried to condense the names into something that rolled off the tongue a little easier, but after two hours, all he had was the acronym W.A.P.B.W.S.U.T., with no pronunciation he could manage. TINSTCTS started off with some promise, but ran smack into a reinforced carbon-laminate hull midway through.

Carousel was what most travelers referred to as one of "the dregs." It wasn't an Earth-like, hadn't been terraformed, but was still habitable—at least at the tropics. Ice caps covered nearly a quarter of the planet, and much of the rest was in a state of near-permanent winter. The equatorial belt hovered in the 5-15°C range, with little seasonal variance, and that was where Carousel's residents clustered.

The *Mobius* arrived at a communal landing field outside the town of Calliope, located on the horse-shaped landmass (if you squinted just right, or were drunk, or both) that inspired Carousel's name. It was a barren, dry patch of land, the native wild grasses trampled under feet and landing gear of countless interstellar visitors. Those grasses got crushed down by a few more of each as the *Mobius* set down and the crew disembarked.

"Back in the cold, dry armpit of the galaxy," Roddy said, the last one off the ship. He took a huge, audible breath and let it out. "And smell that de-icer and coal soot."

"Hey, coal's cheap and local," Tanny snapped. "You don't like it, you can crawl back inside." She climbed into the hover-cruiser the *Mobius* had stolen from the Gologlex Menagerie, shoving Carl out of the driver's seat.

"Thanks, but no thanks," Roddy replied. "I'm finding a bar with a three-meter holovid and an omni link that can get ARGO Athletic Broadcast, and I'm not crawling out until I'm seeing double."

"You coming, Paycheck?" Tanny called to Bryce.

"I thought I'd head into town, look for a solid data terminal," Bryce said. "You know, get started on my end of the deal."

"Nope," Carl said. "You're with us. Me and Tanny talked it over, and we figured we'd trust you on your end. You're meeting Janice Rucker in about ..." Carl paused to check the chrono on Tanny's wrist "... about twenty-eight minutes."

They had talked it over, but it hadn't been some grand agreement. Carl had wanted to trust Bryce just enough to allow him access to a data terminal unsupervised. Tanny didn't even want that much. Janice and her crew were getting the full story, and Bryce was using a hook-up from their local base of operations. The details would get worked out later, since the comm call had only wrapped up while they were on approach to the surface. Carl negotiated with Tanny's nephew Zack, who through the wonders of sprawling, multi-generational families, was two years older than her.

She took the hover-cruiser along the outskirts of Calliope. The buildings were dingy, utilitarian, mostly pre-fab. Aside from places with prominent signage, it was hard to tell corporate offices from apartment complexes, and factories only stood out by virtue of the chemical tanks and smokestacks that clung to them like parasites.

❀ ❀ ❀

The thought of seeing Janice again dredged up old memories. There was the time they had gone to Luna together for a week with Aunt Cerise and had been forced to share a room. Janice had spiked her shampoo with day-glow dye, the same stuff used for construction work to mark off work sites. She had retaliated by adding UV-cured epoxy to Janice's hair gel; it had solidified seconds after she stepped outdoors. Years later, Janice had ratted out Tanny's first boyfriend to her father, lying that Landrew Mitchell had taken her virginity. No one ever saw him again. Tanny was fifteen by then, and her own viciousness had taught her some subtlety. Janice was the subject of a series of nasty rumors that prevented her dating seriously until Tanny left to join the marines—at which point those rumors mysteriously dried up.

The terrain shifted, growing hilly as they made their way through the city. Streets followed the topography rather than conforming to a grid like most colonies. It had an almost Mars-like feel, where the residents preferred natural geography to modern efficiency in city planning. Tanny swung the hover-cruiser through a near-empty shopping district in one of the valleys, then along a natural pass where more low-altitude traffic flowed.

How Janice would react to her arrival, Tanny could only guess. She had come to the wedding, but they had barely exchanged a greeting. A lot of time had passed since their childhood feud—and Tanny, for one, was old enough to consider anything prior to her enlistment to be "childhood." She could only hope that Janice felt the same.

Carl's snapping fingers startled her from her musings. "Hey, I said you missed the turn."

"Sorry," Tanny replied. She slowed and swung the hover-cruiser around in a U-turn.

"Sure you don't want me to drive?" Carl asked. "I can keep this tub under two-hundred," he added, and she could envision the lopsided grin that went along with it without having to turn.

Tanny checked the speedometer and they were only doing eighty. "Nah, I'm good. Just a lot on my mind."

"You just say your awkward little hello, and let me talk to her," Carl said. "In fact, the less you say, the better. Your mother told me the stories of you two spitting and scratching at each other growing up. I bet there's a lot she didn't know, too."

"Probably," Tanny muttered. If Carl was fishing for more bait, he was going to need a less obvious hook.

"This gonna be a problem?" Bryce asked. "I mean, maybe we can just get me to a terminal, and we can meet with your cousin later, once I've—"

"Nope," Carl said. "Well, I mean, yes it's a problem, but no, we're not changing the plan. Janice is family; how bad can it get? Blood's thicker than water, after all."

"What's that even mean?" Bryce asked. "We're not at sea or anything. What's water got to do with it?"

"Hmm. That's a good question. Probably ought to change it up on circumstance. Thicker than opium for narcotics smuggling. Thicker than liquid nitrogen for cryonic kidnappings. Thicker than—hey, what is Janice up to, anyway?"

"Mining equipment, far as I know," Bryce replied.

"Shit. Not sure blood's any thicker than that stuff," Carl replied. "Some pretty dense gear involved in mining."

"It better be," Tanny said. "Or we're in trouble."

"Let's just leave a placeholder," Carl said. "Blood's thicker than somethingorother. Fill it in as needed. Today, let's hope it's thicker than hair gel."

Tanny felt her face warm, and wondered whether it was due to embarrassment or a lack of Pseudoanorex in her system. Possibly both.

There was no holovid to watch, but Mort sat on the couch looking in its general direction anyway. At his side, Kubu took up the remaining space on the cushions, his head resting on his front paws. An empty jam jug lay on its side by Mort's feet, the insides licked clean. Kubu didn't protest when Mort rested a hand on his back.

"Hope you've learned a lesson in all this," Mort said. "A beast of lesser intestinal fortitude wouldn't have survived those poisons you ingest." He made no effort to simplify his vocabulary, unlike the others. Kubu didn't understand complex English any worse than he understood the monosyllabic drivel they cooed at him. Esper was the worst of the lot; she must have told Kubu what a good boy he was a hundred times.

"Kubu's tummy hurts."

"Well, not shit, you Jörmungandrian eating machine," Mort replied. He wondered momentarily whether somewhere on Kubu's homeworld there were myths about a dog devouring the sun to end the world. "Those pills of Tanny's—Mommy's— aren't fit for human consumption, period. Loads of scientific swill, crammed tight as they can pack it into tiny capsules. They're no good for *her*, and she's built up a tolerance to them. You stick to the food we give you, and keep your damn muzzle out of the beer."

"Kubu's tummy still hurts."

"You are a master of conversation," Mort observed. "Still better than Roddy when he's sober, though." He scratched behind Kubu's ears, which caused his tail to start wagging weakly. "*That*, you understand, at least. Things would be so much easier if you could talk. Well, I mean you can *talk*, you just don't ... oh, good Lord, we've been idiots."

Mort extracted himself from the couch, where Kubu's bulk had been resting against him. The canine rolled onto his side and looked up with baleful eyes. "Stay with Kubu?"

Mort was two steps from his quarters when his conscience snagged him by the back of the collar. Kubu whined, and that was that. Such a pathetic, innocent creature, barely able to string three words together. With a sigh, Mort settled back onto the couch and resumed scratching behind Kubu's ears. "You'll feel better before Mommy will, I'll wager. Then, it'll be your job to comfort her. Hopefully, we can have a little surprise for her."

❊ ❊ ❊

Esper strolled the streets of Calliope carrying bags from various food markets. It wasn't the sort of place that warranted strolling, but it had sky and plenty of room for her to stretch her legs. The sky was a dingy grey and the streets dusted with soot and scattered with litter, but she was willing to overlook those facts for the time being. As she walked, she juggled a peppermint soda and a bag of powdered sugar puffs, trying her best not to drop the ship's groceries while she ate.

"This cold is welcome, but the air tastes like ash," Mriy said from just behind her, where she was toting the more industrial foodstuffs that would reload the food processor. Though she carried twice the weight, Mriy seemed to have no trouble keeping one hand free for a ham hock to snack on.

"Is it cold on Meyang?" Esper asked.

"Near Rikk Pa, the best hunting season is winter," Mriy replied. "But the air is clear and the scent of prey carries for kilometers. The snow makes for easy tracking and keeps a flushed quarry slow. Nothing like this place but the cold."

"You can go back to the ship if you want," Esper said between bites. "I can get by on my own."

"Tanny said—"

"Tanny worries too much," Esper cut her off. "Look around. It's a grimy little nowhere town, but it's not exactly New Singapore." There were street vendors and mothers out with children in tow. They had chain restaurants like Choc-o-Barn, Speedy Burger, and Patty Mac's. There were more ground vehicles rumbling along the asphalt roads than hover-crafts above them, but there was enough traffic for the city to feel lived-in. Carousel might have been farther out than most people would consider civilized, but it had the trappings of civilized space.

"Strength is law here," Mriy said. "You won't even carry a blaster."

"I wouldn't fire it," Esper replied. "So why pretend? I'd be more likely to find trouble if I invited it."

"The greatest warrior fights the least," Mriy replied, taking a huge bite out of her ham. "His enemies fear defeat."

"I think I'm better off without enemies, thanks," Esper replied. "I don't mean this as an insult, but you seem ... well, a bit built to force people to have an opinion of you."

"What about that one?" Mriy said, shifting the topic and pointing at a nearby storefront with the remnants of her ham. "They ought to have a holo-projector."

Gladstone Entertaintech certainly looked like a place where someone could buy just about anything. Out in the midst of nowhere, diversion was at a premium. Miners, prospectors, and freighter crews had nothing better to do in their down hours than sedate their brains with drinking and holovids. Some of them, it seemed, might be willing to dump heaps of terras on top-of-the-line gear. "Out of our price range. They probably have holo-projectors that cost more than the *Mobius*."

"Not if you asked Roddy. He seems to think—"

"Speaking of Roddy," Esper said. "Why not guard *him*? Those scrap-peddlers he's dealing with are loads more dangerous than the consumer shopping district. Plus ... you know ... he's little."

"He'll fire," Mriy replied. "And he acts like he'll fire. For him, carrying a blaster keeps him out of most trouble. Few humans would chance a laaku's aim or reflexes."

"Here we go," Esper said. "This place ought to have something I can afford." Randall's Resale was, by all outward appearances, a pawnshop. The window display held an assortment of unrelated goods: a saxophone, a leather jacket, two tennis rackets, an out-of-date EV suit, a rack of jewelry, and several hats. Electronics didn't look like much in a window, but Esper had no doubt in her mind that someone must have sold them an old holo-projector.

Mriy bared her teeth. "Junker."

"We're not rich," Esper replied. "If we want something decent, we're going to have buy secondhand. It's not like something new would stay new long on the *Mobius* anyway." Esper's family had been poor before her brothers left home for fame and fortune. Samson and Napoleon had set up their parents—and by extension, Esper—in a comfortable lifestyle with money they sent back. But Esper still remembered her father bringing home and old broken holo-projector and tinkering with it until the image came in as clear as any off-the-shelf model.

She pushed through the door, setting off an old-fashioned three-note digital chime. Whoever ran Randall's wanted to know whenever anyone entered or left. Esper caught sight of a security camera pointed at the doorway, its little red "on" indicator staring accusingly from beside the lens. The shop was everything Esper had imagined from the outside. Poor lighting. Better for shabby merchandise. Narrow aisles. Made the store seem packed with things to buy. No price labels. Haggling was mandatory.

The chime rang a second time as Mriy followed her in.

"Hey!" a voice shouted. Esper craned to see around the shelves. The man behind the counter was dark-skinned, bald-shaven, with eyes hidden behind red-glowing scanner lenses. "We don't allow their kind."

"Huh?" Esper asked. In the moment it took her to process who the proprietor meant, he clarified for her.

"That fleabag of yours. It'll have to wait outside. Can't have it shedding all over my inventory or pissing on the floor."

Mriy hissed and folded her ears back.

"*She* understands English just fine," Esper said. She made a shooing gesture to Mriy, hoping that she could get the azrin to exit before things escalated. "I'll be fine. Just hold these and wait outside." She pressed her bags into Mriy's hands, thinking that being a tad overburdened might make her less inclined toward aggression.

The door chimed again as Mriy departed, glaring over her shoulder at Esper. "Anything you lookin' for in partic'lar?" the shopkeeper asked.

"Holo-projector," she replied.

"Aisle three."

Looking up, there were indeed plastic-board signs dangling from the ceiling by strings, each bearing a number. Aisle three was next over, and she found another patron already browsing the wares. He was probably a local miner, still wearing his hard-hat and soot-caked jacket. He looked up as Esper approached. Friendly eyes and a leering grin; not a combination she relished in tight quarters. He had bleached sideburns and stained teeth, all nearly the same shade of yellow. From where he was standing, he was on the market for a datapad.

Esper offered a tight, awkward smile, and made eye contact. The probably-miner glanced away and slunk around the corner into another section. She didn't need Mriy hovering over her. She'd been living with such unwanted attention since she was a teenager. Sober and in a public space, perverts were cowards. Putting the encounter out of her mind, Esper scanned Randall's selection of holo-projectors.

They had a Martian Vision 1-meter projector, which was similar to what the *Mobius* had been using before Mort's "incident." It had seen better days, but the model was only two years old, so there was probably a limit to how much wear and tear it could have seen. There was also a Reali-Sim 2655 that went up to 3 meters. They could always set it lower for everyday use, but for special occasions a display area that size could fill half the common room. It would be like living in the holovid.

But something nagged at Esper's mind as she inspected the projectors. On the shelf behind her was a wide array of datapads. She had been using a borrowed one so old that it probably ran on whale oil. The data rate was akin to sending smoke signals, and it could only connect to the omni through the *Mobius*. It was also a little scuffed, and much as she hated to admit it, that fact bothered her to no end. The pawnshop's datapads weren't all pristine, but some were pretty close. She picked up several and handled them, trying to find one that had a comfortable mix of weight (not too heavy, but heavy enough to feel sturdy), texture (smooth, but not slick enough to risk dropping), and color (glossy white was nice, glossy fuchsia or chartreuse would be better).

But money was an issue. Unmarked prices aside, she had a good idea what things would cost, and she'd be lucky if she could get a decent holo-projector on her budget. Getting a new (to her) datapad would preclude any other purchases. And that was when an insidious thought crept into her head.

Datapads were small. She could fit one into the pocket inside her jacket. Cameras were watching, but that was nothing compared to the forcefield at the Gologlex Menagerie; her limited magic had proved more than sufficient to foul that up for a little while. It would probably get the lights too, and the shopkeepers data lenses. The inevitable hunger brought on by her magic use could easily be preempted by eating a couple of the raspberry-peach Snakki Bars she had in her pockets from shopping. She was no Mort. The devices would all be fine in a little while. Simple.

Esper was appalled. She was thirteen the last time she had shoplifted anything; it had been a datapad then, too. Her mother said she didn't need a new one, and that Esper wasn't going to blow all their money on trendy electronics. No one had caught her, and the guilt gnawed at her until she confessed to her priest, who made her return it. A hot wave of shame washed over her, and she set the datapads back on the shelf and left them alone.

Eyes met hers through the shelves. The next aisle over, the miner was watching her again. He coughed—a dry, rattling cough that bent him over at the waist—and looked away. That was the last straw. Esper hurried toward the exit; she could shop anywhere for a holo-projector, but things in Randall's Resale were getting a bit too personal for her liking.

The miner cut her off. "Can't keep your eyes off me, babe?" he asked, resting a hand on one of the shelves as he blocked her path. He reached a hand for her cheek and she slapped it away.

"Get out of my way," she snapped. The miner flinched back, and his jacket swung open just enough for her to see the top of a datapad peeking out of his pocket. He had just been looking at those datapads; obviously he'd found one he liked. Esper gasped. "You're a thief!"

She reached out and pulled open his jacket before considering the consequences. Esper might have felt the temptation, but she dismissed it. Calling attention to the miner proved to herself that she was the righteous one. Keeping silent would have made her complicit.

Of course, the righteous often face consequences.

"Hey!" the shopkeeper shouted. Though he made no move to come out from behind the counter, there was always the hope that he might intervene. And Esper felt the sudden need for a little intervention as the miner put a hand on her collar and shoved her against one of the shelves. She clung to his jacket—stupidly, she realized, but it was reflexive. Overbalanced, he tumbled down with her amid a shower of pre-owned electronics.

"Let go of me, you stupid bitch," the miner snarled. A fist to the jaw set a flash of light behind Esper's eyes. But Tanny's training had developed new reflexes in her, and as soon as her head cleared, Esper brought her arms up to shield her face, and the next blow caught her on the forearm. The miner was atop her and struggling to regain his feet in the unstable pile of plastic and steel electronics casings.

She couldn't let him get away with it—not just the theft, but the assault as well. Too much of her life of late was painted in gray; this was clear, crisp black and white. The right thing was to hold him, stop the thief from getting away, and wait for help. Taking hold of the miner's wrist as he grabbed for a shelf for balance, she called on the universe for aid. Heal him. Speed his metabolism. Cause that stabbing hunger than always comes along with it. Esper didn't bother with the mnemonic rhyme; there was no time for that, and the results didn't need to be pretty.

They weren't.

She had grown used to people doubling over or curling up when their body devoured all its reserves and demanded more sustenance. But the miner collapsed, wracked with agony, hacking and gasping for breath. Esper wrestled to get him off of her, but his convulsions made him too difficult to wrangle. The next moment he went limp and collapsed atop her in a heap. The miner lay still. His warm, dead weight pressed down, threatening to smother her.

All Esper could hear was her own ragged breathing and the tentative footsteps of the approaching shopkeeper. She was afraid to move. Her mind raced with possibilities, but looming over them all was the stark realization that the man draped over her was dead.

"What'd ya do?"

"I... I'm not sure."

"Ya done killed Gerry. And... shee-it, my merchandise is all busted." Footsteps pounded across the room. The slam of a hand, and red lights strobed overhead. A siren sounded.

Esper scrambled out from under the dead miner in the dark as the strobe provided scant help. All she could make out clearly were the door and front windows, where dim sunlight struggled to enter through dirty glass. She burst through the door to find Mriy preparing to go in after her.

"There you are," Mriy said. "What's going on in—"

"No time," Esper said. She grabbed a couple of their bags at random from the sidewalk. "Let's get out of here."

Picking a direction at random, she stopped short. A pair of black-clad security officers jogged toward the pawn shop, stun batons in hand. Mriy tugged her by the arm. "Wrong way."

Reversing direction brought them face to face with a second patrol pair. The four security officers spread out to hem them in. Through the speaker in his black, faceless helmet, one of them ordered, "Get down on the ground."

Mriy dropped their shopping bags, and whipped out a blaster.

"No!" Esper jumped in front of the barrel as the security officers drew weapons of their own. She had no way of knowing whether local law enforcement kept theirs on stun or lethal, but knew that Mriy had no qualms about live fire on city streets.

"Drop the weapon!"

"I said on the ground!"

"Last chance. Drop. The. Weapon."

Though they were surrounded, Esper ignored the officers and stared until she caught Mriy's gaze with her own. The azrin looked away at first, but couldn't focus on the security patrol while Esper's eyes bore into her, welling with tears.

Esper patted the air. "Put it down. It's me they want. I just... there was a... it's all my fault!"

Mriy hesitated, but couched and set her blaster on the ground before raising her arms in surrender.

Esper turned to face her arresting officers. "She's got nothing to do with this. It's me you want. I'll come quietly."

"Subdue."

Two of the officers holstered their blasters while the other two kept theirs out and aimed at Esper and Mriy. Esper held out her wrists and one of them snapped a pair of binders around them. The cuffs pulled her wrists tight together and squeezed until her fingers went tingly.

There was a electrical crackle as another of the officers jabbed Mriy with a stun baton. Mriy growled at the first jab, sucked in a hissing breath after the second, and fell limp after the fifth.

"I told you she had nothing to—"

But one jab of the stun baton was all it took to shock Esper into silence. Spots swam before her eyes, and firm hands grabbed her by the arms as she wobbled.

"Yeah, we heard you."

A second jab and Esper blacked out.

The Rucker Resort was a bold name for a hotel, since most of the galaxy knew of the Ruckers as a criminal syndicate. It was also questionably accurate, since Calliope was a shithole. Unless they had some amazing guest facilities on the *inside*, Tanny was going to call bullshit on the place. Twelve stories wasn't much in a heavily populated area, but out in the fringe of ARGO space it was bloated. It had a flat, gray concrete exterior highlighted with faux neon lighting. On the roof, a small but indiscreet gun emplacement kept it from having that home-away-from-home feel, unless you were from somewhere equally ugly and paranoid.

As a base of operations, though, Tanny had to give them credit. Plenty of room for guests of the syndicate, round-the-clock food service, and no one would wonder about the odd assortment of clientele. It was clever enough that Janice couldn't have been the one to think of it, though there was a good chance she was the one who decided to plaster the Rucker name all over it.

A valet at the front entrance took custody of their hover-cruiser. There was a familiar look in his face, more a type than a specific set of features. Bulging at the seams of a crisp red and gold uniform, he would have looked more at home in a dark alley with a knife. Just inside the hotel, there was someone waiting for her whose features she truly did remember.

He was dressed in an Earth-style business suit with dark glasses pushed up onto his thinning hair, revealing gray eyes. "Good to see you, Miss Tania," the familiar-looking man said, raising Tanny's hackles. Her father's lackeys had always called her that, and despite not recalling the man's name, she had little doubt he'd guarded her at one time or another when she was young.

"Looks like you've come up in the world," Tanny commented. To her mind, it was stating the obvious, but it brought a pensive look to the man's face.

"If you ain't never climbed to the top of a mountain, find one short enough what you can," he replied. Straightening and making a visible attempt to appear professional, he hooked a thumb Bryce's way. "This the guy?"

"Yup," Carl replied. "Bill, meet Bryce Brisson, would-be data-scoundrel-for-hire. Bryce, this is Bill Harker." Carl shook hands with Bill. "Nice place you guys've got here."

Bill shrugged. "Ain't Mars. Hell, ain't even Earth. But we brought a little class to this rock. This guy of yours talk?"

"I... I do," Bryce replied. "I just didn't quite know—"

"Wonderful," Bill said. "You can talk to Miss Janice. I ain't a talker." He turned to Carl. "So anyway, how's that family of yours?"

They crossed the hotel lobby and took a gravity-stabilized elevator ride to the top floor. All the while, Carl and Bill caught up on old times as if they had met more than twice in their lives. Tanny just couldn't understand how he did it. Carl was an imbecile of the highest order on subjects ranging from politics to gambling to basic ship maintenance. But he'd yak for hours with a total stranger until the two of them became the best of friends; he'd remember the poor sap until doomsday. He kept better track of her family and their various goons, lackeys, and middlemen than she ever could. To top it off they all *liked* him... even Janice.

The elevator door opened. "Well, look who Lady Luck brought me today."

The penthouse apartment was decorated more tastefully than Janice's room had ever been back home. Tanny had expected pink everything and plush pillows scattered around just for cuteness' sake. Twelve or fifteen years had changed her cousin that much, at least. The decor was dark and glossy, with a cold look at odds with the 25°C climate inside. Janice lounged on a leather couch, dressed in scarlet. Her crop-top blouse was sleeveless, plunging down her front; it stayed in place by some clever, high-tech fabric trickery. The skirt she wore billowed into individual pant legs as she rose to greet them; heeled shoes clacked on the floor, hidden beneath the fabric.

Carl gave a lopsided grin. "Hey, Janice. Long time."

She swayed over toward them. Gone was the grim jewelry she once wore, as was the skull tattoo that used to grace her left shoulder. Instead she wore a pair of dangly diamond earrings with a matching solitaire necklace against her smooth, clinic-fresh skin. Janice's loose, flowing black hair stood in stark contrast to Tanny's close-cropped cut.

"I forget," Janice said, her attention fixed solely on Carl. "Are you and the princess currently married? I can never keep track."

"Not presently," Carl replied. With not so much as a hitch in her gait, Janice slunk up to him and wrapped her arms around his neck. The ensuing kiss lasted indecently long. It was all for her benefit, Tanny knew. Janice might have gained some class, and learned a bit of subtlety, but she was clearly still new at both.

Janice gasped for breath. "Hello, Tania," she said, her arms still encircling a grinning Carl. "Finally decided to pay a visit? Should have come while we were still on Mars. It would have been like old times."

"Who would've wanted that?"

"My mother, your father, probably a few hangers who still think you're their ticket to the big time, but that's probably about it," Janice replied, disentangling herself from Carl. "No one else misses you."

That last was bit probably an exaggeration, but not by much. Tanny had grown up a lot since leaving home. She could hardly look back on all the things she got away with in her teen years without embarrassment. Dealing with her on a day-in, day-out basis must have been exhausting for most of the family and the household staff, not to mention her security detail.

"Why Carousel? Why Poet territory?" Tanny asked. "Why not just stay cozy on Mars?"

"Cozy?" Janice scoffed. "Same reason you left, sorta. I wasn't anyone's plaything, and I wasn't going to be second string. I put together my own crew, but your father didn't like it."

"Lemme guess, because you wanted to take it outside Sol?"

"No, because your father doesn't trust non-humans in the business," Janice replied. She shook her hair and walked over the expansive windows overlooking the city. The Rucker Resort had a high vantage in the rocky terrain north of Calliope, and nighttime illumination glittered in the valley that spread below them. "All this is mine, just because your father decided to let me go 'crash and burn'—his exact words—trying mixed-raced crews."

"My father's no xenophobe," Tanny protested, unsure why that exact moment felt like the time to show filial loyalty. It probably had to do with the source of the accusation.

"Like *you* know your father," Janice said with a sneer. "Everyone else sees how he is around you. News-blurt: he's not like that with anyone else, not even your mother. Sure, he'll let a laaku do his accounting or draw up contracts, but he's not letting them into the business side of the business, and he sure as hell isn't letting any of the non-primate xenos anywhere near his operation."

Tanny shrugged. "Not a lot of xenos can afford Mars."

Janice snorted. "Yeah, like *that's* an accident. ARGO relocation taxes anywhere in Sol are designed to keep xenos out. But you're traveling with an azrin in your crew, I hear."

"Yup," Carl interjected.

"Figure that makes you at least a few neurons smarter than your old man," Janice said. She drifted over to a side table cluttered with glass decanters and crystal-ware and poured herself a drink. "So tell me about the quiet one. What's he got that I need to hire him?"

Tanny elbowed Bryce. She didn't know if it was nerves or hormones that had his tongue knotted up, but he needed to speak for himself if he had any shot of impressing Janice. There was no confusing her with a delicate flower, despite her current attire. That act fell flat after a minute of her opening her mouth. She didn't abide meekness. Never had. Probably never would.

Bryce cleared his throat. "I'm in data... digger mostly. I know you're in the market for some mining gear; portable, nothing huge, but a good-sized haul in smaller chunks from a fleet set to come through this way. You're set to start a mining colony somewhere bleaker than here; once you've got them though, you're going to want them free and clear, and that's where I can be of use." He stopped to catch his breath, barely having paused in his introduction.

"Jesus," Janice said. "Did you rehearse that or something? Where'd he find out about that job?" she asked Carl.

"Like I said," Bryce said. "I'm in data."

Janice bit her lip as she looked Bryce over for the first time since he arrived. Tanny turned aside so she could roll her eyes without her cousin seeing, pretending to notice the view of the grimy little town below filled with miners and the profiteers who supplied them with a livable world.

"Carl, I got you and the princess separate rooms on the tenth floor," Janice said, picking up a second glass and filling it with an amber liquid from an unlabeled decanter. "Yours has a view of the landing field where you parked. I'm going to have a drink with Mr. Bryce Brisson, and tomorrow he can try his hack to clear your warrants. He has until then to impress me."

Tanny had to learn where her own room was from Bill, who was waiting for them in the lobby. She was tempted to blow off Janice's hospitality and go back to the *Mobius* for the night, but she just didn't have the energy. It had taken all her focus and reserves of strength not to either pass out or vomit in front of her cousin. Instead, she thanked her lucky stars that her room wasn't directly below Janice's and proceeded to do both.

Mort sat beside Kubu, beer in one hand, a copy of *Daedalus and the Art of Artifice* in the other. Roddy had brought back a few essential supplies, along with spare parts for the ship, including several raw steaks. It had only taken two to settle the canine's stomach, but he was still exhausted from his ordeal.

Aside from Kubu's snoring and the occasional mechanical clank from the bowels of the *Mobius*, everything was quiet.

"Mort," Roddy's crackly voice blurted from the shipwide comm. "Hey, Mort ... push the goddamn button labeled 'comm open,' you Iron Age relic."

Mort spared a glance up at the panel, rolled his eyes, and returned his attention to his reading. "You see, boy? There are things about being a wizard. You can't just go letting regular folk drag you around by their gizmos and whatchamacallits. Just you wait and see."

Daedalus and the Art of Artifice was an excellent resource. Mort's copy wasn't original, but it preserved the ancient Greek, making it both informative and a good mental exercise. It provided an escape into a world before technology, when artifice was more a product of imagination and willpower, and less a matter of money and robotic factories. Daedalus wouldn't have built a ship that needed an overhaul after a bit of magic was performed nearby. Then again ... he probably would have built it from a whale carcass with glued-on feathers, so there was a comfort factor to consider as well, not to mention that the *Mobius* passed a lot of suns.

In moments, the inevitable happened. The door to the cargo bay slammed open, and an irate laaku entered the common room. "I *know* you can work a comm panel, you bastard."

"I'm not dropping everything I'm doing the minute you decide—"

"It's Esper," Roddy said. "Call came in from local lock-up. They've got her in on charges."

Mort snorted. "She get picked up trying to shop for Tanny's misbegotten pills? Good Lord, that girl ought to have known better."

"No, murder."

Mort raised an eyebrow. Murder wasn't the sort of thing you could just drop on the floor at someone's feet without explanation. Even snide laaku mechanics had to know that.

Roddy sighed. "She went to some dung-bucket secondhand shop and got in a fight. Other guy ended up dead, and the local sheriff's deputies arrested her."

"I thought Mriy went along with her," Mort said. Mriy's only *real* job around the ship was keeping other people from having to kill anyone—or getting themselves killed.

"She's locked up too, as an accessory."

"I don't see it," Mort said. "Spend five minutes talking with her and anyone with half a wit in his head'll see that she hasn't got it in her. She won't shoot anyone, and she's hardly the sort to break necks. How do they think she killed someone?"

"Cancer," Roddy said.

"So wait, some wretch keels over and they pin it on the nearest offworlder?" Mort asked. "That doesn't make any sense at all."

"They said she used magic on him."

"Bah, Esper can't create cancer in ..." Mort's words drifted, swirling into nothingness as a new thought contradicted what he would have said. He spoke aloud, but to the universe at large, more so than Roddy. "He already had it. She sped it up, same as she speeds up healing. Body's natural processes. What's cancer but those processes run amok?"

"Nasty business," Roddy said. He shrugged and pulled a beer from the freezer. "Anyway, figured you'd deal with it."

"Me?" Mort scoffed. "I'm not a lawyer, and I'm not her captain. Why would they listen to ..." Mort chuckled silently. "Of course. This place is run by pirates. They don't care, as long as someone pays them off."

Roddy cocked his head, pausing mid chug. "You holding out on us? Thought pretty much everyone was scraping terras out of the couch cushions."

"Of course I am," Mort replied. "But that's not the point. Shakedowns work both ways." He stalked off to his quarters to change.

Esper sat on the edge of a cot, chin resting on her hands. A lone, dim panel in the ceiling lit her cell, which was all of two meters by two and a half. The scant light was enough to see by, but allowed the disreputable features of the cell's uncleanliness to remain concealed. There was a toilet and water spigot within arm's reach; the latter didn't work, and she hadn't dared try the former in case it was likewise out of order. The cushion of the cot was some rugged synthetic leather with lumpy stuffing; there was neither blanket nor pillow. All she had were her boots and the form-hugging armor Tanny had insisted she wear in dangerous places like Calliope. Without the concealing shapelessness of the jacket she usually wore with it, she felt displayed, but embarrassment was the least of her shames.

Yesterday she could have said she never killed anyone, and the question would have struck her as preposterous. Now she could not. There was no malice in her use of magic, but she had not known about the miner's illness, nor had she imagined that her healing spell could nurture malignant growths. Kenneth Eugene Shaw. That was the name they had told her, the man she had murdered. Idly she rubbed her hand on the cot cushion, the hand she had touched him with, the hand she had killed with. There was no wiping away the unclean feeling though.

In time, Esper would pray for forgiveness, for understanding, perhaps even to wipe the incident from her memory. But for now she had no business asking anything from the Lord but mercy upon the soul of Kenneth Eugene Shaw, a man taken before his soul had a chance at redemption. Her encounter with him had lasted only minutes from their first fleeting eye contact, and he had left a sour feeling in her stomach. But she had to imagine that far worse than Kenneth Eugene Shaw had been brought back into God's grace. She had denied him the opportunity for salvation. Even if she could forgive herself for causing his death, she could not shirk that responsibility.

She had gotten Mriy arrested, too. Aiding and abetting—what a curious turn of phrase. All she had done was run when Esper told her to run, and drawn a weapon she hadn't used. Had Mriy actually managed to aid or abet, they'd have gotten away. But azrin weren't given the benefit of much doubt. If the sheriff's deputies hadn't known her species, five minutes with a connection to the omni would have been long enough for them to realize she was dangerous.

Worst of all was Esper's deep certainty that she was going to get away with it. The tidal wave of guilt wasn't enough to wash cold logic out of her. Carl was a master of talking his way out of things, and would talk his way around any punishment Esper might be in line for. Barring that, Tanny's cousin was a high muckety-muck in the local criminal clique. Tanny and her cousin didn't get along, but somehow strings would get pulled, someone would owe someone else a favor, and she'd get released.

Esper slumped back onto the bed with her arms crossed. One full wall of the cell was glossy black, mirror perfect. She knew it was see-through from the far side, and that the guards were watching her every second. As a prisoner, she had no expectation of privacy. Even her grief and guilt were subject to the amusement of her captors.

The door opened. "Come on," one of the deputies said. He was the slouch-gutted blond who had told her of the "amenities" when they put her in there, hours ago. His weapon was holstered, and his wrist-restraints dangled at his belt.

"Where are we going?" Esper asked, scooting out of the cell before he could change his mind and seal her inside once more.

"To see the Fleet Admiral."

Esper's head snapped around. Mort stood just a few steps away, dressed in his robes and chain, though he did not have his staff along. Standing beside two more of the Carousel deputies, he showed the sharp contrast between old and new. The local law enforcers had their kevlex uniforms and stun pistols, their bioactivated restraints and their ear-clip comm links. Mort was a peddler of fire and brimstone, a bottomless well of menace with a scowl and two day's unkempt beard.

"You disappoint me, apprentice," Mort continued, wagging a finger at her. "Kill when you must, but kill with intent, not lax control."

"I just—" Esper began, but Mort raised a hand in a curt gesture and cut her off.

"Save it for the Fleet Admiral. I'll not be subjected to hearing the story twice."

"If you'll just follow me," one of the other deputies said. They brought Mort and Esper outside to a waiting shuttle. It was just an old Integra-Cruise Sparrow, but the exterior was painted sky blue with twisting ivy wound about. The painted ivy parted around the vessel's name, the *What Goes Down Must Come Up*.

The air outside was biting, and the armor Esper wore was designed to dissipate heat, not trap it for warmth. One of the deputies handed her back her jacket, and she gratefully shrugged it on as she shivered.

The shuttle door popped open with a hiss of equalizing pressure, and the deputies stepped aside to allow them aboard. Mort slid his hands into opposing sleeves of his robe, never giving the slightest hint that he was cold despite there being no shelter from the stinging wind. He nudged her with an elbow and glared down at her arms, then wiggled his hands inside his sleeves.

Esper hadn't been given much chance to figure out what was going on, but Mort had called her his apprentice—to call that a stretch of the truth was like giving Carl credit for an occasional exaggeration. She wasn't quite comfortable with her own infrequent use of magic, which she had limited to life-threatening emergencies until today, and in retrospect, there had been a life at stake there as well, just not hers. But if Mort had gotten her out of that gloomy little cell (though to give it credit, it was much warmer in there), then she would play along for the time being. It was a snug fit, but she managed to get each of her hands into the jacket sleeve for the other arm.

The interior of the shuttle was partitioned. There was no access for the passengers—herself, Mort, and two deputies—to interact with the pilot. Four seats faced forward, and four others faced them, oriented backward to the direction of flight. Esper sat in a forward-facing window seat, and Mort settled in right beside her. The two deputies, for all their niceties, sat in the opposite corner, as far from Mort as they could get. He set his eyes on them, and with no magic Esper could notice, held them silent in their seats.

There was so much she wanted to ask, but without quite knowing what was going on, she didn't dare. Trust in Mort. It was all she had to go on. If ever there was one of the crewmembers whose plans she ought to trust, it was Mort. Tanny and Mriy were ruthless and might do more harm to her soul than good for her safety or freedom. Carl made up his plans as he went along, regardless what lies he might tell to cover the fact. Roddy, if he were ever to plan anything, the odds of him following through were no better than the flip of a coin—or the pop-top of a beer bottle.

Mort put a hand on her shoulder and leaned close. "Don't worry. I'll handle this," he said, his voice low, but not a whisper. Esper should have been more nervous, but what little doubt she had that she would see this through was washed clean. Was this what magic felt like? Some spell, not even perceptible, just evaporating her worries like dew before the morning sun? If it was, then she could not even blame Mort for doing it. If it wasn't, then she didn't know why it was working. Mort was, by all she had been taught, a tainted soul. Should solace come wrapped in a black robe and bearing the ill-gotten forces of creation?

The shuttle trip was only to orbit. It lasted mere minutes. The sky above filled with a single ship, blotting out more and more stars as proximity altered her view from the window. The What Goes Down Must Come Up was swallowed up by the Poet Fleet flagship. "Welcome to the Look On My Works, Ye Mighty, and Despair," one of the deputies said as the shuttle door opened.

"At least one of these bloody ships is named for a poem," Mort grumbled as he stood.

"Not exactly reeking of humility," Esper replied softly. She followed Mort a step behind and off to his left.

"On the contrary," Mort said. "Read the whole thing sometime. Remarkable sentiment for someone who owns a star system."

The *Look On My Works, Ye Mighty, and Despair* was large enough that there were transport vehicles servicing in the interior. A rubber-wheeled buggy pulled up alongside the *What Goes Down Must Come Up* with a man in a sleeveless gray shirt at the wheel. "Hop in," he said. "Admiral's all curious who the hell you both are."

Esper made eye contact with Mort, who offered a grin and wink, but no explanation. They both climbed into the buggy, and without preamble, the driver sped off. There was no time after that for thinking, worrying, or puzzling, just white-knuckle terror. The sleeveless-shirted driver tore through the corridors of the ship like a rally racer—or like Carl in anything that flew. They had a moment's respite when they stopped in a freight elevator to head up six decks, but then with a squeal of tires, they were off again.

Esper's heart pounded so that she could feel it in her ears, and when she climbed out of the buggy, her legs nearly gave out beneath her. "End of the line," the driver said. He gave Esper and Mort a lackadaisical salute and sped off. There were two officers waiting for them. Esper was guessing at the rank by the way they stood, for there was no uniform or insignia anywhere on their person. One was a woman in her early thirties with a shaved head and spikes through each ear. The other was from a race she didn't know—reptilian, shoulder-tall to his companion, and covered in dull, swampy green scales. If she had to guess his evolutionary origin, she'd imagine he was some Earth-like world's idea of an iguana.

"I am First Officer Hazz Shi," the iguana-like officer said. He gestured to his comrade. "This is Security Chief Indira Jackson. Admiral Chisholm is waiting on the bridge."

Esper found it curious that neither was armed. For the first officer, perhaps it might make sense, but for a security chief to go around without a weapon struck her as out of place. The only way that would make sense was if...

She tugged at Mort's sleeve to get his attention as their escort headed for a the door labeled "A throne is only a bench covered with velvet." He looked down and Esper nodded toward Security Chief Indira Jackson. A twitch a frown graced his brow, but it faded quickly into an understanding smile. A gentle nod confirmed Esper's assertion: Indira Jackson was a wizard.

The bridge of the *Look On My Works, Ye Mighty, and Despair* was luxurious without being ostentatious. The consoles gleamed, with smartly-dressed officers at each station pillowed snugly into leather-upholstered seats. The floor was polished hardwood, or at least appeared so, and beheld a mosaic design in shades of brown. Standing with one hand resting on the back of the command chair at the center of the bridge was none other than the Fleet Admiral.

She turned at the opening of the door. "Welcome. I am Emily D. Chisholm, Admiral of the Poet Fleet." By all appearances, she was no older than Esper, certainly not more than thirty. She wore a jacket and slacks in a checkerboard of jester's motley, tailored to her tall, slim form. At her neck she sported a ruff like a Renaissance nobleman, and she wore her dark hair dangling over it in pigtail braids. For the moment, Esper was at a loss for words.

"Charmed," Mort replied, sketching a shallow bow with his arm across his waist. "I am Mordecai The Brown, former holder of the Eighth Seat of the Convocation and Guardian of the Plundered Tomes. And this is my apprentice, Esper Theresa Richelieu."

Esper ducked her head in an emergency bow, caught unprepared for Mort to take on her introduction as well as his own. "Ma'am," she mumbled.

"I am a great admirer of the truth," Admiral Chisholm said. "It is as scant a resource in this galaxy as any gem, as any piece of artwork. In return for receiving so precious a gift as unblemished truth, I could forgive a great deal."

"What do you want to know?" Mort asked. Esper felt a knot of dread as to what Mort might say if he let loose with *too* much truth, and worse yet, what Admiral Chisholm might do if she caught either of them in a lie.

The admiral turned her attention to Esper and her face brightened in a condescending smile. "Are you truly his apprentice?"

Esper swallowed and shook her head.

"I thought not," Admiral Chisholm said. "The Esper Theresa Richelieu that I dug up was a priestess initiate of the One Church. I highly doubt such a dichotomy of soul exists that would allow one woman to serve such opposing masters. Certainly not a dead woman. Tell me, did you fake your death or steal Sister Theresa's identity?"

"Faked," Esper admitted. "I'm not proud of it, but I ruined my career in the clergy and... well, at the time it seemed like a good idea."

"And *you*, Mordecai Brown," Admiral Chisholm continued. "Are you the same Mordecai Brown who is wanted by the Convocation for a sum that temps even me to violate the hospitality of the Freeride System?"

"You wouldn't survive the attempt," Mort replied, lifting his chin. "If you like truth, let *that* one stick in your craw. We're here about that little scuffle in Calliope, not to trade threats."

"Very well." Admiral Chisholm took a step toward Esper, who flinched back a half step. "The miner had an untreated malignant tumor in his left lung. "You caused the rapid growth of that tumor until it killed him in a matter of minutes. Do you deny this?"

Esper shook her head.

"Do you *deny* this?" Admiral Chisholm snapped. "Answer me!"

"No," Esper said, looking down at the exquisite floor and imagining herself crawling beneath it.

"Are you a wizard? Was that why you faked your death?"

Esper shook her head and realized that wasn't going to be enough. "No. I just know the one spell."

"Why would you claim she was your apprentice?" Admiral Chisholm asked Mort.

A sly smile crossed Mort's lips as he paused before answering. "She won't get it out of me that way."

Esper's puzzlement momentarily overcame her shame. "What do you—"

Admiral Chisholm waved a dismissive hand. "Indira, enough. I don't know how you managed it, but she can't even contact me telepathically. Your reputation doesn't do you justice, Mordecai Brown."

Mort offered a helpless shrug. "You get out into the galaxy, you learn a few things. Those pointy-hatted old fools back on Earth must think my brain's gone to rot out here, but I get to practice an awful lot of *not* doing magic. Your Indira seems like a nice enough girl, but she's got all the ego of an assistant janitor. Universe isn't going to listen to her when I've got my boot on its throat. Sorry, if you two had a 'thing' going that I interrupted."

Admiral Chisholm's eyes brightened. "Excellent segue. Speaking of things that are going, that is the crux of the reason behind Miss Richelieu's arrest. I don't give a miser's pity about some thieving local miner, but the Rucker family is operating in *my* territory. I want to know why, and I want them dealt with."

"But you own this whole system," Esper protested. "Just kick them out."

Admiral Chisholm tapped a finger to her lips. At first Esper took it as a shushing motion, but quickly realized that the admiral was thinking. "There is, of course, that option. But I don't want Don Rucker to bear me ill will. Should any blood relative of his be harmed in the eviction, I would be looking over my shoulder till the end of my days. Better to work through an intermediary. Janice Rucker has some scheme at work here. I don't know what it is, but she's far too settled on Carousel for my liking. Miss Richelieu will be staying here until Janice Rucker and the rest of the Rucker Syndicate are out of Freeride."

Esper felt the hair rise on the back of her neck. Mort stepped forward, placing himself between the admiral and Esper. "I don't think so."

"I do," Admiral Chisholm replied. "You're going to go back to the surface, inform your captain of my terms, and use whatever wits you have to get Janice Rucker to leave Freeride. Until then, Miss Richelieu will enjoy the hospitality of the *Look On My Works, Ye Mighty, and Despair.*"

Mort squinted at Admiral Chisholm. "You don't look worried that I might just kill you where you stand."

"An act," the admiral admitted. "I've never tested my anti-wizard defenses against one of your presence."

"Mort, don't," Esper said, pulling him back by the arm. "I'll stay. Just ... fix this." She turned to the admiral. "What about Mriy?"

"I've already offered her a job," Admiral Chisholm said with a shrug. "She turned it down, and has been returned to that heap you so generously describe as a ship. Now, take your leave, Mordecai Brown. Miss Richelieu will come to no harm aboard my ship. Even should you prove unsuccessful, she will merely ... remain."

Mort nodded slowly and put a hand on Esper's shoulder. It had a warm, comforting weight. "All right. If you're willing to play along, I'll leave you with these... poets." Esper could only guess that he almost said "pirates" and thought better of it. He turned to the admiral. "If she *does* come to harm, you can bet I'll be back to test whatever traps you may have set up in here. Oh, and I appreciate the Shelley reference."

"So few do," Admiral Chisholm replied. With a flick of her fingers, the door to the bridge opened. The man in the sleeveless shirt waited outside, his ground-car idling a few meters down the corridor. The door closed behind Mort. There was a brief squeal of tires, and then she was alone, surrounded by genteel pirates.

Tanny paced her room at the Rucker Resort. It was a tenth-floor suite looking out on the ice-capped mountains to the North, but the glare from the holovid ruined the night view. The fight between Graccio and Martinez had seemed like a good plan to settle her mind. It was just a middle-weight bout; there was no title on the line, just distracting violence to numb her worries. The cool marble sucked feverish heat out through her bare feet, and her pacing kept the floor from warming in any one spot.

A knockdown in the fight momentarily captured her attention as the announcers went wild and the unseen crowd cheered. Graccio would have been Tanny's bet if she'd been inclined to place one, but he wasn't long for the fight by the look of things. Just one more bit of evidence that she was off her game. Normally she was the one to pick the winners when she and Mriy went to the fights in person. Mriy was good at sizing up azrin fighters, but Tanny was better at evaluating humans.

He was late. When Tanny had discovered that Janice hadn't put any restrictions on in-room communications, she had immediately gotten on the local section of the omni and dug until she found someone who could help. It had taken a debit against her future pension from the marines, but she had gotten a hold of enough digital terras to place a discreet order for some illicit chemicals. It wasn't everything she needed, but it was better than what she had. But that was two hours ago, and it should have taken her contact less than half that time to make the drop-off.

A melodious chime had Tanny rushing for the door. Thoughts of strangling the courier for making her wait were swept away in a floor of relief. She hammered the door release with her thumb. It snapped into the wall with an audible whoosh. As she opened her mouth to make a snide comment, she froze.

Bill was standing there, a rumpled brown paper bag in his hands. It looked out of place against the backdrop of his tailored Argozzi suit. "Good evening, Miss Tania. We had a delivery for you down at the front desk."

Tanny snatched the bag from Bill's hands. "Thanks." She pressed the door control once more, but Bill put a hand in the entrance, triggering the safety override that kept guests from getting slammed in doors.

"Miss Tania, didn't you learn nothing all them years with guys like me looking after you?" Bill asked. "You looked surprised to see me, which means you didn't check the security screen to see who it was. Could be it was anyone out here."

Tanny glanced to the screen by the door. It hadn't even occurred to her to check. Either she was getting used to the P-tech all over the *Mobius*, or she was getting sloppy. "I didn't want it recorded," she lied. "It's none of Janice's business who I see."

Bill held up his hands at stomach height, just enough not to be intimidating. "And Miss Janice don't care, neither. But it's all on recording, all the time, just in case—you know, nothing special in this case on account of it being you and all. Gotta tell you, we ran that shit—pardon my Earthy tongue—ran that junk through the chem scanner, just to be safe."

Tanny waved a hand in a circular motion. "And?" She wanted this conversation over, and Bill stumbling over himself wasn't getting any of the drugs into her bloodstream any quicker.

"Miss Tania, that tweaker who brung this stuff ... this is some serious stuff, you know?"

"Yeah," Tanny said. "I kinda knew that. I don't care, as long as it's all in here."

"Um," Bill said. He reached a finger inside his shirt collar and tugged. "You see... I can't lie to you, Miss Tania. I had to take some of them pills out."

"Which ones?" There were a few in her order that she could live without—in the literal sense, probably any of them. But she had already worked out in her head what the makeshift cocktail would do to her. Re-figuring what she could and couldn't afford to ingest wasn't part of her evening's plan. Drugs. Shower. Bed. That was all she was looking for, with emphasis on the bed.

Bill took a step back. Tanny could have snapped the door shut between them if she hadn't wanted answers. "Just the Cannabinol."

"What?" Tanny shouted, not caring if anyone heard, or if the security cameras had an audio feed that might pick her up. "God dammit, Bill. That was the one I was *really* hoping you weren't going to say. Plus, of all the fucking things ... seriously? That shit's harmless compared to the rest." Cannabinol would calm her, and more importantly settle her stomach to keep her from vomiting up the rest of her purchase. In fact, until it had time to kick in, she wasn't planning on touching the rest.

"Hey, I made your dad a promise a long time ago to keep you off that kinda stuff," Bill said.

Tanny reached out, grabbed Bill by the collar, and hauled him back into the room. "Listen to me, Bill," she said quietly, her face centimeters from his. "I spent eight years in the marines. They gave us stuff to keep us on top of our game. I've been taking it all this time, even since I've been out. Look me in the eyes. Right now, I'm dry on all but the *one thing* that will let someone my size snap your neck like a dry twig. But I like you, Bill." She let go of his collar. "So I'm going to let you go downstairs and bring back that Cannabinol. NOW!"

In a back room behind the hotel bar, there was a gathering that wasn't open to the general public. The chairs were high backed, cushioned like a dream, and gathered in a circle around a table strewn with cards, chips, and glasses of booze.

Four holovids played around the room, all sports, but no one was watching. It was all just atmosphere. The room Tanny's cousin had provided was nice enough, but Carl felt more at home surrounded by people.

"Hey, look who be back," Mikey Whistles hollered, grinning with his gap-toothed smile. Bill slouched and shook his head as he lumbered in.

"Told you," Carl said, draining the last of a bottle of Amberjack Ale. He tossed a taped-shut cardboard package to Bill, who snatched it from the air with a scowl. Carl pointed around the table. "Pay up, boys. Bill can lie his ass off all he wants, but that girl's getting high tonight or killing someone." No sooner did he set the bottle down, but one of the waiters scooped it up and replaced it with a fresh, cold one.

There were grumbles around the table, but a mix of chips and hard-coin terras made their way into Carl's pile, turning barrel-scrapings into a proper hoard. Carl pulled it toward him, just enough to make room for cards to settle in front of him. He might stack them; he might not. It all depended just how fast he started losing them.

"How'd you know?" Janice's cousin Veronica asked. She wasn't family to Tanny, being from Janice's mother's flock, but she had a coincidental resemblance to Tanny in her build that Carl was finding harder to ignore, bottle by bottle. "You'd think he coulda slipped one past her."

Two-Shot Pete chuckled from his belly. He hadn't lost so much as a terra betting on the ruse. "You ain't known Carl long enough, then. I think no one's got Princess Tania figured out but him."

"Maybe we just pity bet him," Gazlir said with a sharp-fanged smile. He was azrin, with ash gray fur and the tip of his left ear missing. He had given Carl a growl when introduced, and when Carl laughed it off, he had earned a bit of the azrin's gangster's respect. "Since his rusty ship's falling apart."

Carl laughed despite the sting. "Oh, that one hurts. Cheap shot, taking aim at my ship. Behind his back, no less. You come on board sometime and talk shit about *Mobius*." Carl pointed an accusing finger at Gazlir, using the hand that held his beer.

Bill slunk away to go deliver Tanny's Cannabinol as the poker game went on. Carl was determined to at least hang onto enough for a used holo-projector by night's end. All he had to do was play safe and... there was a second thing, but after four bottles of Amberjack Ale, he couldn't think what it was.

"Why you loopin' 'round the borderland in that heap, anyway?" Mikey asked. "Don would'a taken you any day of the week—twice on Tuesday."

Carl tipped his chair back and held up his hands. "What can I say? Tanny won't budge on it. If it were just up to me, I'd be wearing a cheap suit like Gazlir's and using terras to fill my swimming pool." He pointed to Gazlir, whose sleeveless suit probably cost as much as an engine overhaul for the *Mobius*. But he had to give the guy *some* grief for disrespecting his ship.

Two-Shot Pete raised his glass, half filled with twelve-year-old scotch and two ice cubes. "To Carl, the most henpecked, love-struck son-of-a-bitch between here and Andromeda. I'd put myself in front of a blaster bolt for Tania Rucker, and I wouldn't blame Carl one iota if he was the one who fired it."

"Here, here," a chorus echoed around the table. Glasses, bottles, and tankards clinked and clanged. Carl chuckled. There were times when he wondered...

The shush of the door sliding open brought Esper awake with a start. The unfamiliar surroundings confused her for just a moment before she remembered her circumstances. Security Chief Indira stood in the doorway. "Good morning. I trust you slept well."

Esper pulled up her blanket, feeling underdressed in the nightgown the Poet pirates had provided. Her cell—if it could remotely be called that—was nicer than her quarters on the *Mobius*. In fact, it was nicer than her room back home on Mars, because whoever had decorated it had refined taste. It wasn't the frilly, garish explosion of self-expression from a girl whose parents had decided to give her whatever she wanted. The floor was wood-inlaid, warmed from beneath and polished to a shine. Her bed was four-posted with heavy velvet curtains on all sides. Books lined shelves on one wall; windows that looked out over the planet below took up most of another.

"Um, yes," Esper replied. "Fine, thank you." The mattress had been a pillow for her whole body, so soft she had felt weightless.

"Dinner to your liking?"

"Delicious," Esper confirmed. They had given her a menu, and she had picked everything chocolate that the kitchen had. It had been a day that warranted something sweet.

"And Raimi?"

Esper flushed. She had been preparing for bed when Raimi had arrived. He wasn't tall, but had arrived bare chested and glistening, with a smile that shone like pearl to offer his services. There had been a fair amount of beating around the bush before they settled on a massage being among her options. She had been skeptical at first, putting herself in the hands of a half-naked man, but Raimi's fingers had worked any lingering tension from her muscles, like a magic all his own. It had taken a fair bit of praying to keep her from suggesting any more than that.

"He was nice," Esper said, and cleared her throat. "So ... what now?"

"Your clothing is being laundered and will be returned to you," Indira said. "However, you will have a wardrobe provided by this afternoon, at the admiral's direction. There is a bathrobe in the washroom if you feel a chill in the meantime. Breakfast will arrive shortly. You may amuse yourself however you like. The holovid is omni-connected and has an extensive in-core library of classical works. Most of the books are written in English. So long as you handle them with care, you may read any you like."

"And ... that's it?"

"That's it. You are our guest for the time being."

"Not that I'm complaining, but why treat me like I'm staying in a New York Prime hotel?"

Indira's face grew stern. "Admiral Chisholm believes that Mordecai The Brown has more than a passing interest in your well-being. The cost of pampering you is insignificant compared to the risk of angering that one." The security chief's lip curled in a slight smile and Esper caught a twinkle of mischief in her eyes. "And besides, you have a soul filled with grace and a form pleasing to the eye. You fit in well here. I think I may enjoy looking after you."

Esper was not sure she had stopped flushing from before, but felt the blood rushing in her ears. She was beset by hedonists.

The planning room for what was being called the Operation RIBBIT looked like an executive board room that had been vandalized. It had the signature long, glossy black table, but it was covered in take-out containers and the chairs were a hodgepodge of different styles. All around the walls, there were posters for the Lewiston Black Barons, ad sprawls for popular holovids from the past few years, and a flatvid that flashed sports scores and betting lines from major events around the galaxy. Below the flatvid was the motto: "It's always game time on some world."

Carl sucked in the whole atmosphere in the few seconds it took for the door guards to let him and Tanny through. Mort was already seated inside, looking grumpier than usual, along with the rest of Janice's crew. "Good, you two are the last. Rudi, clamp down the door so we can get started." The door guard complied, and the conference room was sealed with an ominous thud.

"First things first," Carl said. "How'd our boy do?" The effort of trying to sound chipper fell flat. He was buzzing on too little sleep, a hangover, and three cups of coffee. He tried to tell himself he was wide awake and feeling fine, but for once he wasn't buying his own bullshit.

"You should be a squeaky-clean, upstanding citizen in a couple days," Janice replied. She had exchanged the slinky attire of the previous night for a black button-down blouse and slacks. One could have easily mistaken her for a legitimate businesswoman. "My guy, Marty, circled him like a vulture the whole time and gave him the all clear. If Bryce has the connections he claims, it's down to the waiting."

"How's he ride?" Tanny asked in a voice like lead. Unlike Carl, she was looking much better this morning, though he had noticed a look in her eye that disquieted him. When they met in the hall a moment earlier, she had looked right through him. He usually earned himself a glare or a frown or even a quick averting of the eyes to pretend she hadn't seen him.

"Excuse me?" Veronica spoke up. "That's no way to talk to Janice."

"This is business," Tanny said. "I want to know if we're bringing Bryce along because we can use him or because he can light you up. I saw you weighing him with those eyes of yours."

"You're out of—" Veronica began, but Janice cut her off with a raised hand.

"No, it's a legit question," Janice said, staring down Tanny like a gunfighter before a shootout. "I gave him a shot, but hey, he's a family man." She flicked a hand through her loose hair. "Says he kept them out of his official record, but he's got a wife and two kids. A new bed warmer might have been nice, but a family man's always a more reliable business associate."

The words hung in the air as Tanny and Janice glared at one another.

"So," Carl said. "I hear the holo-projector in here's top of the line."

"Yeah," Mikey Whistles said. He fished in his pocket for a remote and turned it on. The unit was mounted to the ceiling directly above the conference table, and the field hung in the air at the center of attention. "Boom! How's that for resolution? Smooth as ice."

A small fleet of ships appeared in the air, hanging in formation. The two-dimensional text markers all appeared to be facing Carl, though he knew through some techno-trickery it was making it look that way for everyone. The fleet was labeled: "Roy, Barnum & Toyoda Mining Expedition." The R, B, and T were highlighted, and below, the words Operation RIBBIT, with the R, first B, and T in matching blue.

"Here's our job," Janice said, pointing to the fleet as she began to walk around the table. Carl slid into a seat before she had to go out of her way to walk around him. Tanny did likewise, scowling at Janice instead of watching the holo. On the table, one of the boxes still had some cold spicy chicken wings, and Carl helped himself to one. "This is the Roy, Barnum & Toyoda law firm's side business. One of those stuffed-suit Earthers got it into his head that the Platt System is ripe for an unregistered mining colony. Low profile. No paperwork. Real hush-hush. I only got the system name out of them when I said I couldn't bid unless I knew where I was going."

"So we're working *with* the mining lawyers?" Tanny asked.

Janice snorted, clearly amused with the appellation. "Something like that. They hired me—that is, us—to provide security in ARGO's absence. We get them there, hang around a couple days while they get settled and cozy planetside, then we get paid two hundred grand."

"What are they mining?" Mort asked. It was unusual for Mort to take an interest in operational details. It must have been the secrecy that gnawed at him.

Mikey spoke up. "Sssssure don't know," he said, letting the long, sibilant 's' whistle. "Them boys is tight on that lock. They won't say. They people won't say. All's we know is it's gonna be a mint."

"So, they're just mining... somethingorother?" Carl said, waving his hands in little circles as if he was searching for the word.

"Don't matter none to us," Mikey said, grinning.

"I take it we're not going to Platt?" Tanny asked.

"No siree, Miss Tania," Mikey replied. He gestured to Carl with a beckoning finger, and Carl passed the cold wings.

"The mining fleet has three armed vessels," Janice said. She poked her finger into the holo-field and ships glowed at her touch. "Delta-grade military surplus. All obsolete. All retrofits. Just guns welded onto the outside of heavy freighters, really. It's mostly a deterrent. Once we get out of secure space, *we're* their protection." Janice gave a smug grin that she shared around the table. There were nods and chuckles, but Carl knew a humoring-the-bosslady chuckle when he heard one.

"So where do we come in?" Carl asked. "Looks like your crew's got this covered."

"You brought me Bryce," Janice said. "He gets to clean up the registry on those vessels so I can resell them half legit. He flies with you; he's your responsibility. Since this is his first job, he gets a half share, and you and your crew can split the other half as a referral." She looked to Tanny. "Don't let anyone say I never done anything for you."

Carl furtively did a count around the table, trying to parse out how Janice would be splitting up the spoils with her own gang and estimating what one share was worth. That was when he remembered that it wasn't two-hundred grand that was going to split, but the profits from the stolen ships. At that point, he gave up.

The meeting delved into boring details on the ships, their crew complements, their defenses and weaknesses. Carl's eyes glazed over, and the dim light let him nod off through much of it. He knew his part. He owned a ship that was going to babysit a data-wrangler. Tanny would be flying it, and Mriy could handle the turret if it came to that.

Carl woke from his not-so-covert nap with Mort's hand on his shoulder. "Come on, Van Winkle, time to head back. There's something we need to talk about before Bryce finishes up here."

Tanny's mind was flat during the ride back to the *Mobius*. They had a ship to get back into shape, supplies to stow, and gear to purchase before they departed. Her thoughts were on none of that. Carl blathered away to Bill, who piloted the hover-cruiser for them, a conversation filled with his usual inanity. She paid it no heed. Mort stewed beside her, hunched in his sweatshirt and grim as she'd ever seen him. That warranted a passing inkling, but she had more pressing concerns: Janice was dragging them into piracy, and she was struggling to be bothered by that.

Tanny knew she didn't want to cross that line, taking her money over other peoples corpses out in the Black Ocean; it had been a hard rule she and Carl had agreed on when first putting together a crew for the *Mobius*. But she hadn't been about to get her hands on any Sepromax from her on-world contact. The little weasel, Branson, she had scrounged up as a supplier carried marine pharmaceuticals for buyers like her, but Sepromax wasn't standard issue; in fact, it ran counter to one of the marines' primary uses of Recitol. She *knew* she didn't want to murder a bunch of innocent spacers in order to steal their little mining fleet, but she couldn't actually care about it.

It was a frightening thing, realizing the control a drug can have over you, even as it tightens its grip. She wasn't afraid of getting caught. Odds seemed good they'd get away with the crime. She wasn't scared for her safety. It was as easy a job as they'd had in months. A lazy part of her brain said it wasn't worth arguing over and that she might as well get paid for once. It was only that memory of her resolve not to fall prey to the amorality side effect (if it truly wasn't intended by the chemists, which she questioned) of Recitol that kept her from caving.

The plan needed to be simple. It needed to be lazy. If she got frustrated or overwhelmed, Janice's Operation RIBBIT might just seem like the path of least resistance. Get back to the ship. Supplies. Repairs. Sneak off world when no one was looking and trust Mort to keep them below astral sensors. There would be hell to pay for it someday, but it was a price Tanny was willing to pay, she was pretty sure. It was hard to tell, when she couldn't give a spent fuel rod about the fate of those mining colonists.

The hover-cruiser arrived at the *Mobius*, leaving Bill to take a local shuttle back to the resort. She might have muttered a goodbye before he left, but a minute later she couldn't recall.

"Come on," Mort snarled through gritted teeth. It was odd for the wizard to be the first back aboard ship. Hurrying was one of a laundry list of activities that were beneath a wizard's dignity, according to him.

"How's the repair job going?" a chipper Carl asked Roddy as the laaku closed the loading ramp behind them.

"Good as you can expect, given our budget," Roddy replied with notably less enthusiasm. "Mort catch you up on what's gone on while you were in Ruckerland?"

"No," Mort snapped. "I didn't. I got a grand total of the walk up that blasted ramp without some drooling Rucker lackey dangling his ears in my way. These ninnies even let one fly us back here; Mr. Hangover and Mrs. Chemical Imbalance were in no shape to operate a hovery-wagon."

"Something I need to know about?" Carl asked.

"We can't do it," Tanny blurted. She shook her head both to clear it and for emphasis. "We're not pirates."

"Wait. What now?" Roddy asked.

"Yes, we are," Mort replied. "That's what I needed to tell you."

"You guys turned pirate since yesterday?" Carl asked. The look of bewilderment on his face would have amused her if she were capable of it at the moment. Instead, all she felt was a rising irritation. Unfortunately, anger, annoyance, and impatience were all quite intact despite the Recitol.

"As if Esper would have gone along with that," Tanny said.

"Actually, Esper's *with* the pirates," Roddy said.

Carl held up his hands for attention. "There's no way ..."

"Of course not," Mort said. "Esper's *with* the pirates. She isn't one of them."

"Why is she with the pirates?" Tanny asked. No one was making enough sense for her liking, and she wasn't certain that her off-kilter brain chemistry was the least bit to blame.

"There was an incident," Roddy said. "Esper and Mriy were out picking up supplies. Some dipweed local starts trouble, Esper kills him, Mriy gets beaten bloody, and the pirates took Esper."

Carl made a switcheroo motion with the index finger of either hand. "I think you flipped that around. Mriy killed someone, and Esper got roughed up."

"Nope," Roddy replied, crossing his arms and looking smug. The laaku was clearly enjoying this.

"Enough!" Tanny shouted. "Someone start making sense. I'm going to break a neck every time someone starts a story in the middle and leaves out the essential details. Starting with yours." She leveled a finger in Roddy's direction.

Roddy cleared his throat and backed in the direction of a toolbox. As if that would save him. "Mort. You tell 'em."

Mort described the events that had led to their being arrest and Esper's subsequent transfer to custody on the Poet

Fleet's flagship. The killing being a magical accident and Mriy being subdued by a dozen armed sheriff's deputies added the necessary plausibility to quell Tanny's rising anger. The involvement of the Poet Fleet crystallized into focus: local politics. You just couldn't let folks inhabit star systems in numbers greater than a dozen or so without them fracturing off into factions and creating politics.

Tanny turned to Carl. "So it's the room that's cursed. It's not just tech specialists on the *Mobius*. It was always both until now."

"We're not leaving her," Mort said. Tanny had expected the first reaction to be Carl's, and had already prepared herself for an argument against him.

"I mean," Tanny replied. "How long have we really known—"

"Tania Louise Ramsey," Mort shouted. "Whatever gremlins are clogging your brain, you should be ashamed of yourself."

"Easy, Mort," Carl said, patting the air. "Tanny's not herself today. Cut her some slack. No, we're not leaving Esper."

"But we said 'no piracy,'" Tanny said softly. They weren't listening. She was *trying* to keep it together. Right and wrong were fuzzy enough just then without Mort and Carl changing the rules. "Years ago. We ... we won't be like my father. We've got standards."

Carl took a long, steady example breath, and Tanny followed suit. "It's going to be OK," he said. "We're going to get Esper back. We're going to get paid. Yes, maybe there might be something resembling piracy involved, but you heard your cousin ... that fleet belongs to lawyers."

"Well, shit," Roddy said. "Lawyers? Practically doesn't even count as piracy, does it? I mean, who're bigger crooks than lawyers?"

Tanny suspected they were having one over on her—there was too much grinning. But she couldn't put a finger on the hole in their logic. They were stealing from lawyers, whose job mainly consisted of using the law to screw with people. They would use law breaking to screw with them right back. Stealing their ships and killing the crews would serve them right.

"All right," Tanny agreed. She aimed her threatening finger at each of them in turn. "But you're not fooling me. This is piracy. But we're only going to do it a little."

"It's not like we can just knock off a ship or twelve, swing back to Freeride, pick up Esper, stuff our hands in our pockets and walk off whistling," Carl said, keeping his voice low. He leaned against the window of Mort's quarters, his back to the landing field. In the unlikely event anyone had a camera on them, they wouldn't get his half of the conversation by reading lips.

Mort rubbed a hand across his face as he paced. "Well, I don't see any paths except through the darkness. Esper's familiar with the concept of repentance. We can apologize afterward for resorting to wanton murder to save her."

Carl sighed and let his head loll back, wincing when it thumped against the glassteel. "I just get this nagging feeling that she might take that apology, then have us leave her in the first civilized place we come to. She still sees a lot of blacks and whites."

"Well, piracy's pretty black territory even if you're fluent in grays."

"Point taken."

"Tanny's going to be put out, too, once she gets herself right," Mort said. He shook his head. "This is worse than the usual stuff you slip past her—I mean any of us."

Carl shook a finger at Mort. "This would be a lot easier if you had just rescued her instead of letting them take you both up to see Admiral Chisholm."

"What? You think I expected them to hold her hostage?" Mort asked. He paused his pacing and held up his hands to the sky, unseen through the ceiling and the hull of the *Mobius*. "This was all supposed to be a meat-fisted shakedown. She gets arrested on a bullshit charge when she was clearly the victim of an attack. I go up with her to see whatshername with the funny costume and Oxford vocabulary. She tries to shake us down. I tell her who I am. She blanches. I waggle my fingers and give her the squint-eye. She lets us go and apologizes."

"Well, your plan came off flawlessly."

"You can't tell me I haven't pulled that one off just like that a time or twelve," Mort said. "Besides, it was refreshing dealing with thugs who name their ships after Shelley and quote Napoleon over their doorways."

"Up until they said 'we're keeping Esper, now get the fuck off my ship,'" Carl said.

Mort nodded. "Yeah, that was about the point they lost me. Bugger me if that girl might not have really *had* some defense against wizards on that bridge of hers. Wasn't willing to risk it, not with Esper right there."

Carl frowned at Mort. He wasn't generally prone to overprotectiveness. "You and Esper really aren't..." He bumped his fingertips together. "...are you?"

"Yes, Carl," Mort said dryly. "I've seduced our resident disgraced priestess. The one who's younger than my own children and covers her eyes when there's nude scenes in a holovid."

Carl shrugged. "Prudes are the ones who snap and go wild. You gotta admit she's sort of drawn to you."

"It's the magic, not me," Mort said. "You never thought much of it, but she likes the feel. Mark my words, that girl's going to fall, and fall hard, from that One Church dogma of hers."

"Hard enough and soon enough to break herself out of a modernized Hades-class battlecruiser?"

Mort twisted his mouth aside in a puckered frown and scratched his chin. "Not likely."

"Then I think it's time we got ourselves used to the idea of kicking my dear ex-cousin-in-law out of the system," Carl said. "Once we figure out how."

Tanny lay on her bed cockeyed, her neck limp, head upside down over the edge. The windows on her side of the ship looked out at the mountains, which resembled nothing back home on Mars. They were dark gray crags jutting out against a lighter gray sky. A world washed free of color, just like the insides of her skull. There was an odd sense of detachment, knowing that her emotions were drowning under an ocean of chemicals whose exact workings went far beyond her understanding. She should have felt horror, she knew. But she wasn't horrified. Horror was an emotion that those chemicals had punched in the gut and thrown out an airlock.

As she stared, she heard her own breathing, and that of Kubu, sleeping on the floor beside her. Tanny tried to take stock of what she could still feel and what was numb inside her. Anger—yes, that she had felt already. Fear—even the

Sepromax only partially brought that back; she was bone dry. Trust—that much was working, since she had taken Carl and Mort at their word. Surprise—she could think of no way to check that, but would watch for it if something came up. Disgust—she tried to picture Carl sleeping with Janice, but felt no reaction. Arousal—well, she wouldn't be perpetuating any species anytime soon. Sadness—she thought of Chip, Gandy, Maxwell, and a dozen other friends she'd lost in war or otherwise, and brushed a tear from her eye when the mountains outside grew blurry. Happiness—that was the big one. That was quality of life. There were different kinds of happiness. Blasting the last lutuwon drop ship out of the sky and whooping it up with her fellow marines was nothing like the simple joy of playing in the dirt as a girl on Mars.

It wasn't a happy day. She'd planned a pirate raid on a mining fleet and heard that a friend had been kidnapped. That was another emotions she'd check on when circumstances allowed.

Kubu yawned and looked up at Tanny, his face upside down to hers. It was an awkward reach, but she twisted an arm around to pat him on the head. "Kubu's glad to have Mommy back. Kubu loves Mommy." He nuzzled his head against her hand.

Tanny felt a twitch in her face. It was a smile. "Looks like that works. At least a little. Mommy needed that."

Tanny staggered out of her quarters in search of food, stretching to loosen tight muscles. She hadn't planned to fall asleep. It had just happened and not in the most comfortable position. Kubu followed at her heels, his repeated query of "Food?" told Tanny they were thinking the same thing. It was a worrying thought, that she had been reduced to the mental simplicity of a semi-sentient canine. Hopefully once they were both fed, the gap would widen.

"Hey, sleeping beauty," Carl greeted her. "We were getting ready to draw lots to see who'd have to kiss you awake. Looks like Kubu got to you first." He was sitting at the kitchen table with Mort, playing their stupid holographic monster game as Mriy and Roddy looked on, clearly bored.

"Nothing personal," Roddy said, perched atop the back of a chair. "But I wouldn't have done it. Those kids' stories from Earth are all sorts of fucked up."

"Sorry," Tanny replied. "I'm feeling a little more myself now. I think the worst is over." 'Little' was the operative word. She was a little optimistic, and the thought of Carl naked was a bit more arousing, but everything was muted. Her feelings were on the other side of fogged glass; she couldn't touch them, and she could only make out indistinct shapes for most.

The fridge was restocked, and sometime during her nap, Roddy had repaired the door. There was plenty beer, a better selection than they usually stowed, but nothing fancy. She pulled a six-pack of Moudren Pale Ale and checked to see what sort of sandwich the food processor could assemble for her.

"Hold still, boy," she heard Mort say. Tanny turned to find the wizard bent down in front of Kubu, with his back to the rest of the crew. He was whispering something to the dog, but she couldn't make it out. Kubu didn't seem to mind, whatever it was.

"What are you doing over there?" Tanny asked across the room. She glanced to the food processor controls and punched in a quick BLT. It was a light meal, but enough to keep her from getting drunk on an empty stomach.

"One second," Mort replied. "One... more... second."

Kubu yelped.

"Kubu!" Tanny shouted, "Are you all right?" She was startled to realize she was concerned about him and startled a second time when it occurred to her that she could be startled.

Mort stepped away, a smug grin on his face. Tanny hurried over as the processor grumbled, working on her lunch. Kubu pawed gingerly at his ear with a hind leg. "What did you do to Kubu's ear?" Kubu asked.

"Everyone," Mort said, "Say hello to Kubu."

"What do you mean?" Carl asked. "He's been here weeks now."

"Whatever," Roddy muttered. "Hello to Kubu."

"Why are we greeting him?" Mriy asked.

Kubu's eyes went wide and his jaw hung open. He stopped pawing at his ear, stood, and took a step back.

"Mort..." Tanny said. "What did you do?"

"You... you can all *talk!*" Kubu said. He craned his neck to look up at Mort. "You made everyone talk?"

"Shit," Carl said. "Those earrings work on dogs?"

"Why are we working bullshit jobs out in this wasteland when we can just sell those to dog owners on Earth and Mars?" Roddy asked.

"They don't work on dogs," Mort replied. "It does seem to work on whatever Kubu is, though."

"All this time..." Tanny said.

"Yup," Mort replied.

"I could have been bitching his ass out for shitting in the cargo hold."

"Any chance we can teach him to use a toilet?" Roddy asked.

Kubu stared from one speaker to the next, the same gape-eyed wonder in his eyes. "So... crazy..."

"Kubu," Carl said. "You know what we're saying?"

Kubu nodded enthusiastically. "Uh huh."

"If we showed you a magic water-filled hole that you can shit into, then push a button to make the shit go away, think you could manage that?"

"You can do that?" Kubu asked. "Kubu thinks that's the bestest thing ever!"

Carl turned to Roddy. "Sounds like a 'yes.'"

Tanny crouched down beside Kubu. "My name is Tanny. You can call me Mommy if you want, but Tanny is my name. And I want you to eat only food, not just anything you find."

"I'll teach him the controls for the food processor," Roddy said. He thumped a fist against the machine.

"Kubu can make food in the big noisy?"

Carl shrugged. "Sure. Saves us the trouble of feeding you."

"When did you figure this out?" Tanny asked. Mort had kept secrets before—he probably still had more than the rest of them combined—but this felt out of character for him. Letting an animal shit all over the ship as a joke seemed too crude for his humor.

"Only really came to me yesterday," Mort replied. "But I got sidetracked. Then I figured I could wait until Tanny got back so she could see him understand his first words. We got to spend a lot of time together while you and Carl were holed up in the luxury of Casa de los Bandidos."

Roddy chuckled. "I was thinking of the Rucker Resort as more of a Seroki Jyzak."

Everyone just looked at Roddy.

"What?" he asked, balancing on the chair back and raising all four hands in a uniquely laaku shrug. "Seroki Jyzak ... from *Temple of the Scoundrel Mutant Prophets*. You all watched it with me. How could you forget a thing like that? The brothel that was a front for the Fifth Hand assassins."

Tanny shrugged.

"I liked that holovid, but I didn't pay attention to the details," Mriy said. "The Leaping Masters were good fighters."

Carl cleared his throat. "Once they introduced Master Gojeth's human sidekick, I was mostly watching her. You may have noticed I have a thing for tough girls."

"Anita Shau is a joke in laaku films," Roddy said. "Her accent is pitiful. They dub over her for the Phabian market. She's just there to get human eyeballs on the holos. A holo with a human in it makes twice on Earth what it does back home."

Kubu spoke softly. "Tanny? Mommy? What are they talking about?"

Tanny leaned down and replied low enough that none of the others would hear her. "Nothing at all. They talk a lot just to hear themselves. It's OK to ignore them."

Kubu nodded.

It was going to be a different world for him now. Tanny wondered how he would adapt. It gave her a moment's pause to wonder how Esper was faring in her own new world, as a prisoner. A little knot formed in her stomach. Things were coming back, and she wondered whether she was better off *not* feeling them.

Esper turned a page, relishing the sound of paper sliding against paper. Most of the books she'd ever handled had plastic pages, and the few paper books she'd seen were deemed too precious to touch. But she was growing accustomed to the faint musty smell, the texture of the pages, the curious weight. She had chosen *Oliver Twist* from among the pirates' eclectic library and was nearly finished with it. Time passed more quickly between the pages than it did in the throes of a holovid stupor. Besides, recent circumstances aside, she could watch holovids any old time. This was an opportunity.

The door warning chimed. Whoever was outside would wait ten, perhaps fifteen seconds for her to disentangle herself from any compromising position she might be in, then barge inside. It had been fairly consistent in the three days she had been 'held' aboard the *Look On My Works, Ye Mighty, and Despair.*

Esper set the book on the side table and looked around. The chair's abundant cushioning had engulfed her, forming around her delicate posterior like a mold. Her feet, propped bare on the ottoman in front of her, had tiny balls of cotton wadded between the toes. Each toenail bore a fresh coating of burgundy paint, still smelling of the alcohol-based evaporating agent as they dried. She hadn't painted her fingernails yet, loath to lose the reading time as she waited for them to dry before handling rare and valuable books.

Raising her hands in a helpless gesture, she waited for the door to open. She was simply in no position to get up and greet anyone.

"Miss Richelieu," Cormack said when the door opened. "The Admiral wants to see you." He was her favorite among her keepers—they hardly seemed to be guards. Fair hair, neatly cropped. A soft, high voice that could have been called prissy. He stepped inside as if hesitant to disturb her.

"Well, this is her ship and all," Esper replied. "But she picked an inopportune time." She waved a hand at her toes.

Cormack smiled and gave a knowing wink. "You have time. She's invited you for dinner. She expects formal dress."

"Let me guess..."

Cormack nodded.

Esper sighed. "Fine. She wins."

The very afternoon of her arrival, they had provided her a simple dress, cut almost perfectly to her size. It was a child's picture book image of what a dress should be and as blue as a crayon. It had just been a placeholder. After obtaining proper measurements, some madman tailor aboard the *Look On My Works, Ye Mighty, and Despair* had made her five more. Not a one of those five could have been described as plain. It was a far cry from Tanny's policy of functional, practical, inconspicuous clothing.

But there was one that had clearly been the formal option.

"Dinner will be at 19:30 Earth Standard Time," Cormack said. He set down a datapad and Esper's heart quickened. A datapad meant contact with the outside world. "I see the look in your eye, Miss Richelieu. It's a datanote. No omni, no comm. All it contains are dressing instructions and a reminder alarm. Sorry."

"A girl can hope," Esper said with a sigh. She liked Cormack. He seemed to understand. A dinner with him, she could have looked forward to. Someone she could talk with, laugh with, maybe take her mind off not being allowed to leave. And she could flirt with him until she was old and gray and never get him to like women. "How bad is it?" she asked, glancing from the datanote up to Cormack.

"You'll be stunning," he said. With a flippant, playful salute, he took his leave. Before the door closed, Esper just caught a glimpse of the *actual* guard, a thick-armed fellow with a stun baton clipped to his belt.

Her current attire was the nightdress she'd been given her first night in the pirates' custody. It seemed impolite to chance ruining a new dress with nail polish, even if she was technically a prisoner. Extracting herself from the cushiony nest she'd formed in her reading chair, Esper plucked the cotton balls from her toes and found the nails to be dry. The room's wardrobe was imitation Earthwood, oak grown on some arboretum world. She couldn't imagine even Admiral Chisholm could afford the real thing.

Inside the wardrobe, there were five dresses on numbered hangers. The Poets were the most detail-oriented pirates she'd ever heard of. The datanote's instructions made it clear that Dress 5 was the proper attire for the evening, though the included pictures made it impossible to confuse with the others. Checking the antique style hands-and-number-wheel chrono, she deduced that it was nearly two hours until dinner. She had time to paint her nails, take a long bath in the hot tub, and snack on chocolates in case dinner was something fancy and inedible.

By the time she was ready to dress, Esper had resigned herself to her fate. Dress 5 was a puzzling mix of the formal and risqué. Admiral Chisholm knew Esper had been a priestess, and had clearly passed the notion on to the ship's dressmaker (Esper still couldn't fathom anyone joining a pirate fleet in that capacity). The fabric was a somber black; it was smooth and soft without a trace of shine, trimmed around the edges with a few millimeters of white silk. There was black embroidery that only showed upon close inspection, swirling in patterns of ivy around a crucifix nestled over the stomach. From a meter away, it was all but invisible against the black fabric. The inside of the dress was all white silk and felt wonderful against her skin. It stretched a little as she pulled it up; there were no clasps, no zippers, not even one of those trendy self-sealing polymerized seams. It simply stretched as it went over her hips and snugged in against her waist once it was past.

There was a full-length mirror beside the wardrobe. The fabric came just high enough over her breasts that she could be shown on a family-friendly holovid feed, but no higher. Esper bounced and twisted, worried that she might have an unfortunate accident, but the dress clung to her modesty. It was like a chaperone that only allowed sex after a nice meal. The skirt came to her knees in a flare of petticoats, but left her lower legs bare.

"Computer, five more degrees, please," Esper said to the room, and she heard a whoosh of warm air begin flowing in to counter the chill that was more in her head than on her legs.

The datanote wasn't done with her yet. There was a silk neck ribbon specified as well. After that, in the top of the wardrobe, a black cloche hat with a white bow. The matching shoes were sixty millimeter heels, and Esper wobbled around the room for a few minutes getting used to them. She hadn't worn heels since she was eighteen.

She hadn't removed either her crucifix necklace or her bloodstone charm, which had turned a shade of pink that would be embarrassing if anyone recognized it for what it was. The color stood out against her pale skin—the only touch of color in her ensemble. Leaving it behind seemed foolish. The last thing she needed was weeks waiting for it to attune itself to her again if she was late in putting it back on.

The door warning chimed. It was time to go. Her escort was the thick-armed guard, who barely spoke a word and looked her square in the chest when he did. It was high school all over again. For a few minutes, once she had worked out the kinks in walking in heels, she had posed in front of the mirror like a glamor model, feeling ladylike and pretty for the first time in a long while. Thick-arms had turned her back into a piece of meat in an instant.

The admiral's private office was up a short metal stairway. Esper clung to the railings with an iron grip as she tiptoed in her heeled slippers, the soles so new they might as well have been waxed. But her relief at the top was fleeting, replaced by wonder.

They were at the top of the ship, in a clear dome, either glassteel or transparent metal, depending on whether science or magic had been used. Stretched out above them was Carousel. It was a dull, ugly world compared to many, but stretched out and filling the sky, it was breathtaking.

"I'm glad you like the view," Admiral Chisholm said. Esper blinked and turned her attention to her host and warden. Her eyes went wide, and her tongue stuck in her throat. The admiral had changed out of her uniform and into a dress better suited to sleepwear than receiving company. It was flimsy, diaphanous, and held up by two thin strips of fabric. The admiral's hair was unbound, still wavy from having been in braids. She wore a pair of gold-rimmed spectacles perched on her nose and held a wine glass.

Esper's first step cost her a stumble, her attention fixed on Admiral Chisholm and not on remembering to keep her toes pointed down. "Sorry," she said as she grabbed the edge of a side table set with a platter of cheeses.

"It becomes you," Admiral Chisholm said. "Even if you're not used to it. Go ahead. Ask. I see the question in your eyes. There can be no truth where questions are feared."

"I feel overdressed," Esper said. She made a gesture as if to point, but stopped short of actually aiming a finger at the admiral. "You... you seem rather relaxed, admiral."

"This is a place for getting out of yourself," she said, flourishing her wine glass. "For you, it's getting out of the drear and drudgery of your self-imposed life as a spacer. For me, it's getting out of prim and proper and being called admiral. In here, please call me Emily, Esper." She gestured to a seat across from her.

"Thank you... Emily," Esper replied, sinking gratefully into a seat and sneaking her feet out of her heels. How had she worn those to school every day for years on end?

A crewman in something resembling a tuxedo slipped in and poured a glass of wine for Esper and refilled Emily's glass. Esper sipped it, and found it more sweet than biting.

"If you are wondering about the occasion, I have good news for you," Admiral Emily said.

Esper pursed her lips into a dutifully expectant smile as she lowered her glass. She cocked her head.

"The data specialist you brought with you to Carousel is a mole. My people dug into his ... well, details are boring, but he works for an anti-syndicate task force. All your friends need to do is get themselves out of the crossfire, and the Earth Interstellar Enhanced Investigative Org will take care of Janice Rucker for me."

"So, I can leave?" Esper asked. She took another sip of the delicious wine.

Emily gave a sniffing chuckle as she drank, then wiped her mouth with a finger. "No, not yet. But soon enough, should your friends not get swept up in the whole affair."

Dinner came, and it was unlike anything Esper had eaten. Despite her family's rise to wealth and respectability, it had always been a secret shame that her parents had clung to low-class cuisine, preferring the taste and familiarity to the more stylish selections of their newfound peers. Esper had never eaten duck, let alone one basted in Earth-wine sauce, and her apple was infused with chocolate, a feat she had never heard of before.

Throughout the meal, Emily questioned Esper about her personal philosophy, and how one went about living within the teachings of a single school of thought. In return, Emily shared her commingling of Machiavelli and Augustus Caesar's views into the command of her own fleet.

"It's not as if I earned respect instantly," Admiral Emily replied. She waved a fork for emphasis, a bit of duck skewered on the end. There was a slur in her voice, not enough to sour its melody, but enough to suggest a saturation with wine. "I was handed the fleet from my father, who had gotten it from his mother. First I Machiavelli'ed the ones who refused to follow me... not suitable for dinner conversation. Then I set my sights on building, expanding, conquering. Do great things. Taking Freeride... all my idea."

Esper couldn't recall who Machiavelli was right then, and Caesar was the one who got killed in Shakespeare as far as she remembered. "That's impressive. Very impressive. You have the nicest bunch of pirates I've ever seen. And I've seen..." Esper frowned a moment. "...two."

Emily laughed, and Esper found it infectious. Crewmen came and cleared away their dinner plates, and refilled their wine glasses. Esper knew she'd drunk too much, but it tasted so good she was having trouble finding a reason to refuse more.

Emily took a long swallow of wine and sighed. It was the sort of emptying sigh that purges the lungs to leave you feeling clean inside. Esper grinned, and Emily locked stares with her. "You know," Admiral Emily said. "I might enjoy spending a night in my own quarters." She licked the wine from her lips.

Esper giggled. "It's your ship. Who's going to tell you where to sleep?"

Emily stood and dragged the fingers of one hand along the table as she came around to Esper's side and stood behind her. Esper felt the warmth of hands on her bare shoulders and the whisper of breath on her ear. "Those are my quarters you're borrowing. I wouldn't think of imposing where I wasn't... wanted."

Esper blushed head to toe, and her breath quickened. This had suddenly become a sticky situation, with the risk of becoming stickier. The good idea/bad idea portion of her brain was submerged in a liter of wine. She was pretty sure there was sinning on the way—not that drunkenness wasn't a sin already. A lot of sins seemed to be chasing her down of late, and Esper was doing a poor job of sidestepping this one. Compared to murder, it seemed fairly minor. But that had been an accident, and this one might also be an accident. She hadn't had a man in her bed in six years, and this wouldn't even technically break her streak. Not to mention the other night when she'd had her engines revved up to full throttle before diverting emergency power to a harmless massage.

Esper stood, stumbling to her side and catching herself on the edge of a table with a helpless giggle. Emily bent down and looked her in the eye, laughing along. "I'm... I... flattered, but I... I can't."

Emily hadn't received the message any more clearly than it had been transmitted. "Sure you can. It's eeeasy. I can show you." She reached out and put her hands atop Esper's.

Esper pulled away, catching herself on Emily's chair. "No. Not 'no,'" she said, holding up her hands to ward off hurt feelings, then grabbing hold of the chair once more when wine and heels threatened to deposit her on the floor. "But it's a... philosophical thing. Core principle violation."

Emily straightened and sighed again, this time wistful. Her drunkenness seemed much less pronounced as she walked over and laced her fingers behind Esper's neck. "Such a shame. I had assumed, since you shunned Raimi—"

"Nope," Esper said, shaking her head emphatically, causing a sudden wave of dizziness. When the spell passed, Emily's lips found hers. She struggled briefly in her surprise, but the taste of sweet wine and the warm softness relaxed her. Alarm klaxons horned in her brain, warning of error codes and improper signals being received. Esper closed her eyes.

Emily released her with a gasp. "A pity. Your soul is a work of art. If your friends didn't make it back, I'd have gladly kept you as my personal attendant." With that, she turned and headed down the stairs.

Esper made the walk back to her borrowed quarters barefoot, leaning on Thick-Arms for support.

❀ ❀ ❀

As soon as the door closed behind her, Esper collapsed against the adjacent wall. The room spun as she leaned her head back until it bumped against the faux plaster with a dull thump. With a push of willpower, she abandoned the support of the wall's presence, and let her heeled shoes drop to the floor as she staggered toward the dessert cart, freshly replenished in her absence.

Her stomach sloshed with wine, still being sucked into her bloodstream and her liver, continuing to exacerbate her drunkenness. If she didn't act quickly, she'd pass out, losing goodness only knew how much vital time. The *Mobius* crew was walking into a trap, and she was the only one who both knew and was inclined to inform them. The pastries were probably delicious when savored one by one, teasing out flavors from frostings and jellied fillings. Rammed into her mouth in pairs, with more to follow before she finished swallowing the prior lot, it was a sugary mush.

When the nausea of overeating threatened to overwhelm her, Esper used her magic. "Cuts close, bruises fade; three weeks healing done today; bones knit, pains ease; cleanse the body of disease." The rhyme was a comfort, a measure of control she had lacked when she killed Kenneth Eugene Shaw. The warm giddiness of her alcoholic stupor gave way to the fevered heat of her bodily functions kicking into overdrive. In seconds, the confusion of drunkenness had passed, along with the overfull sensation of a stomach crammed with jelly-puffs.

Bryce Brisson worked for the Earth law enforcement. Janice was being set up, and everyone was going to get fished up in the same net if she didn't warn them. She needed a way to contact them. Her first thought was the datanote on the table. Sure, they had *told* her it was limited to just a few select functions, but the easiest modification to a standard datapad would be to just lie about what it could do.

It was a Tooky-brand datapad, which didn't bode well. If anyone was cheap enough to sell datapads with all the functionality of a few slips of paper, it was Tooky Industries. The menu options were limited, letting Esper see the dress she was still wearing, along with a diagram of suggested accessories. It had an alterable alarm set for fifteen minutes before dinner, but which wasn't helpful in any other way she could imagine. There were standard functions as well: a calculator, calendar, a number of selectable background images, but nothing that transmitted.

The application of a butter knife was enough to pop the case open, the front and back halves popping neatly apart. The innards only took up two thirds of the interior volume, the rest being wasted space. Esper pored over the components, identifying each part as she was able. Processor. Screen. Microphone. Data Storage. There wasn't even a camera or motion sensors, let alone a broadcast antenna. She pushed the pieces off the table in disgust.

She had already checked the holo-projector, back on her first night with the Poets. It was a receiver only, and she knew she didn't have the know-how to convert it into a two-way. That left finding a transmitter somewhere else aboard the *Look On My Works, Ye Mighty, and Despair*. That meant getting out past the guard. Or did it?

The guards were regular crewmen. They were full-on pirates, with loot and plunder, probably. They could afford fancy clothes and shiny weapons that could do all sorts of interesting and horrible things to people. Her door guards only carried stun batons—which was a small comfort, not that she wanted to get beaten with stun batons—but the other Poets carried a creative array of weaponry. People who can afford expensive things don't carry around Tooky datapads; they'd have top-of-the-line OmniWalkers or Slashcubes, maybe one of the trendy laaku Yinswoos.

Esper stopped short. It was the second occasion in the past week where she'd considered stealing a datapad. "I must have some hang-up on datapads," she muttered. "I should probably buy myself a nice one when this is all over." That seemed like a reasonable compromise. Head off theft by indulging in palliative consumerism. Not quite a biblical solution to the problem, but that was a matter for later prayer and introspection.

A quick check of the wall chrono said it was nearing midnight. "What?" she gasped. She had dined and snacked and drank with Emily for hours. She felt a small pang of guilt for apparently leading the admiral on for so long. It was more effort than anyone had put into seducing her in a long time. But the late hour meant that a change of guards was due at any moment. Thick-Arms would hand her over to Paul, one of the few whose name she had learned.

Her hands shook. They knew what she was thinking before she even admitted it to herself. After cleaning up the broken datanote, she poured herself a glass of champagne. She hadn't touched the room's stock of liquors until just then, not wanting to turn into Roddy, who washed away his time in a liquid coma. But she was fully sober, and a sober Esper wasn't what her plan called for. She downed a half glass in two giant gulps, then refilled it halfway and took a seat in her reading chair. The hat got in the way of her lounging, so she tossed it on the floor nearby.

The door warning chimed. Her heart quickened. The plan had flaws, not the least of which was that of its several resolutions, the successful paths were all a choice between minor evils. She took another quick sip of champagne to dull that little voice that told her maybe her plan wasn't supposed to work.

"Good evening, Miss Richelieu," Paul greeted her when the door opened. "Anything you need, I'll be right outside until morning." He stepped back into the hall, and was about to close the door.

"Wait!" Esper said. "There is something." Paul stepped back in and put his hands on his hips. He was rugged, squarish in the shoulders and jaw, with a shaved scalp and pecks that showed through the fabric of his shirt. Esper licked her lips and avoided looking Paul in the eye, but let him see her looking over the rest of him. "Do you have a moment?"

"Sure." He looked over his shoulder, then hit the door control. They were alone together.

"What are your orders, specifically?" Esper asked.

Paul shrugged. "Keep you from going anywhere. Not let anyone in without the admiral or Indira's say-so. Pass along if you need anything."

"What if it was something you could do yourself?" Esper asked.

Paul shook his head. "Can't leave my post. I can get someone to bring you anything, pretty much. What do you need?"

"Are you breaking your orders right now, then?" Esper asked. "You're not outside the door."

"I can be in here," he said defensively. "Ain't nothing wrong with that."

"Long enough for drinks?" Esper asked. Oh God, please let her not sound like a blithering idiot. "Maybe... longer?"

Paul smirked. "I heard about you and the admiral tonight."

Esper swallowed, wishing she were a teensy bit more drunk for this. "A girl has needs, but it's... well, some locks just need the right key." Dear Lord, had she just said that? Where did that come from? Was it from some sappy holovid? Hopefully Paul hadn't seen it if it was.

"Oh yeah?" Paul asked, his smirk turning speculative. Men were such docile brutes. Esper fought back a wave of disgust over just how easy this was proving to be.

She stood and eyed the wet bar. Tipping back the remainder of her champagne, she asked, "Care to fill me up?" She waggled the empty glass. That line she recognized the moment it escaped her lips. It was from *Daisy's Choice*, which she had watched more times than she cared to admit.

Paul was subtle, unhooking his stun baton and setting it on the table by the door. Nonthreatening. He knew that much, at least. He apparently knew the selection in the admiral's quarters as well, picking up an unlabeled decanter without hesitation. It was obviously not his first romp in this suite.

As he poured, Esper slipped around behind him, dragging a hand along the rippling muscles of his back. From the corner of her eye, she could see Paul's grin widen. But in her other hand, Esper held an unopened bottle of Chateau Descartes 2648; she brought it down on the back of Paul's skull with all her might.

Paul grunted and keeled over, stumbling to a knee. Esper hit him again before he recovered. He fell limp, and Esper breathed a sigh of relief, mixed with horror. She crossed herself, closed her eyes, and asked forgiveness. There was just no other way she could think of to save her friends. Sleeping with Paul *might* have worked, but she had chosen her lesser evil and she was going to stick with it. Besides, it was easier than sneaking around, hoping he didn't wake up.

Paul kept his datapad in a pocket at his thigh. Even limp, the muscle was stiff. Esper caught herself admiring his physique, but quickly shoved those thoughts aside. She had been right; his datapad was modern. It was an OmniWalker Tudor, last year's most popular high-end model—not that Esper had followed such trends, or quietly envied the Harmony Bay scientists' children who carried them. It was thumbprint locked, which proved to be an impediment for all of ten seconds. Paul limply obliged from the floor.

Tanny's safety drills came in handy once more. Esper had memorized the comm code for the *Mobius*, the one that didn't show up in general directories on the omni. She punched it in and waited.

There was no response.

Frowning, and wondering why no one was answering when she really needed them to, she keyed the speaker override for the shipwide comm. Anyone on board would hear her now. "Hey, someone answer. It's Esper." She hissed out a frustrated breath. "Mort, if you're there, just push the red button below the speaker. Red. Speaker. Right below. Just push it and talk."

Mort could be dense about technology at times, but she *knew* he could work the comm panels. She was drawing a deep breath to shout through the ship's speakers when a voice came through the datapad.

"Kubu push button."

Esper nearly dropped the datapad. Her eyes went wide, her hand limp.

"Kubu good? Hello?"

"Kubu, find Mommy... Mo-mmy. Get Mommy." She could only hope he would go find Tanny for her.

"Mommy's not here," Kubu replied, his voice coming through admirably clear over the excellent speakers in the OmniWalker Tudor. "Everybody went out. Kubu can't go. Kubu is guarding the flying house."

Esper blinked. He understood her. That was a reasoned, direct reply to her command. She had to be sure. "Kubu, you can understand me?"

"Yes. Who is this?" Kubu asked.

"Esper. Mommy's friend. You know me."

"The one who puts flower smells in her hair?"

That would have been her lilac shampoo. Good gracious, he *did* understand her. "Kubu, do you remember the new person? The one with short hair who sleeps in the front room?"

"Yes. He hides from Kubu."

"Kubu, you need to tell Mommy that he's a bad man. He works for..." She knew Kubu could understand her, but she doubted he was quite up to relaying 'Earth Interstellar Enhanced Investigative Org' in any cogent manner. "He works for the people who want to put Mommy and everyone else in a cage. He plays tricks on them, and he's not nice. You need to tell Mommy. Do you understand?"

"New man in front room plays tricks on Mommy and wants to put her in a cage," Kubu replied.

This was too bizarre. She was talking to a dog, and entrusting him with a mission. "Can you remember that until Mommy gets back?"

"Yes. Did you know Mommy has two names? Mommy's other name is Tanny." Kubu sounded so proud.

Esper swallowed past a lump in her throat. "You're a good boy, Kubu." She hit 'end call.' Quickly deleting the call record, she locked the datapad and slipped it back into Paul's pocket.

There was still a limp body on the floor beside her. It was time for the unpleasant part of the plan.

It took all her strength to drag Paul across the floor. If not for the polished floor, she might not have been able to manage at all. Admiral Chisholm's suite was equipped with a hot tub, and she left him at the edge of it. She turned away as best she was able and began removing Paul's clothes. But there were buckles and snaps, laces, and parts where she had to wiggle him around to get garments out from under his dead weight. There was just no ignoring him completely. She scattered his clothes around the bed as if they'd been discarded amid passion.

Paul's naked form was distracting. He was warm and a tad sweaty, not sliding along the tile floor around the hot tub nearly so well as he had across the hardwood. It took her nearly half an hour to wrestle him into a seated position in the hot tub. Turning on the water, she took a long breath and prepared for the embarrassing part. As the tub filled, she stripped off her own clothes and likewise discarded them by the bed.

Not looking at Paul was nearly as good as him not looking at her, and she covered herself with her hands despite being, for all practical purposes, alone. Admiral Chisholm was not the sort to deny herself girlish pleasures, and there was a selection of bubble additives. With a wince, she found one labeled in pink with claims of aphrodisiac properties. That was the right one; she had to play it up as best she could. As the bubbles filled the hot tub and the breeze from environmental controls chill on her bare skin, Esper crossed herself and climbed in opposite Paul.

It was a small hot tub, just large enough to be intimate with two or for one to relax and sprawl. Esper did neither. Even below the water level and bubbled, she covered herself with her hands, just on the off chance Paul woke. There was no getting away from touching him, either. Her legs ended up tangled with his, and there wasn't much to be done about that. Except wait.

An hour passed, then another. Esper had to reheat the water several times and refresh the bubbles once. The little jets of water were the only consolation—they felt wonderful on her back and legs. At long last, a few notes from an unfamiliar song blared muffled from Paul's pocket. It repeated, over and over, for a minute or more, then ceased. Paul hadn't answered; it was only a matter of time until someone came to find out why.

The door warning chimed. Esper was already touching Paul—she'd had quite enough of touching him, actually—so it was a simple matter to heal the wound she had inflicted. He began to stir just as another of the guards barged in.

"Paul, what the *fuck* you doing in there?" the guard demanded. A pillar-necked thug, he was the sort that most seedy organizations in holovids kept around to rough people up. The guard held a datapad up to his mouth. "Yeah, he's in here. He's been sticking it to the admiral's girl. ... Yeah, no, he's *right* here in front of me. ... No, you'd never know she was a priestess. Just get a couple guys down here, I'll take a picture and show you later." He took his datapad and angled it toward Esper.

Esper ducked as far down into the water as she was able, but Paul was taking up much of the free space.

"What's going on?" Paul demanded.

"I'm sorry," Esper said, loud enough that the guard with the datapad was sure to hear. "I didn't mean for us to get caught. You fell asleep. You got a comm on your datapad. I didn't want to wake you."

"How did I... did we... we didn't just ...?"

Esper nodded. It was easier lying without saying the words.

"Come on, lover-boy," the guard said, striding over to the hot tub. Esper hadn't planned this far ahead. She scrunched into a ball as the guard loomed over them, but all he did was grab Paul by the upper arms and haul him out of the tub.

"I... I..." Paul didn't seem to know how to put his evening back into a shape that made sense.

"Put yer clothes on," the guard said. "I don't give a shit if you're wet, I don't wanna drag your naked ass through the ship."

"Please," Esper said. "You don't need to tell Admiral Emily—I mean Chisholm. I... I don't want her to take this the wrong way."

The guard shrugged. "The admiral's a fine piece of lady. If that ain't your taste, that's your business. But really... this sorry scab was your back-up plan?" He looked to the floor shook his head. "'Who ever loved that loved not at first sight?' I get, but Paul?"

Esper kept her eyes averted as Paul dressed and the new guard escorted him away. Sleep couldn't come soon enough to put the day behind her.

Bryce Brisson strutted into the common room of the *Mobius* like he had just won the ship in a poker game. Fresh haircut. Clean shave. He carried a small footlocker by one handle, slung over his shoulder. There was a grin on his face as he shook Carl's hand, and he clapped Mriy on the shoulder as he walked by. He had a nod for Roddy and a wink for Tanny. He seemed about to pat Mort on the back as he passed, but a stern look from the wizard made him abort the attempt. Tanny tried to envision him undressed and was pleasantly surprised to find she liked the prospect.

She was feeling more like herself—her old self. Days spent in planning sessions with Janice's crew brought back memories of her time in the marines. Sure, her cousin's little splinter syndicate was nowhere near as hard-nosed and gruff as the 804th Planetary Insertion Division. But she felt a familiar rush of anticipation, like the hunger before a holiday feast.

"Quarantine looks like it treated you well," Tanny remarked. None of them had seen Bryce since Janice took custody of him, but with the mission launch coming up, he was entrusted to the *Mobius* once more.

"I've drunk more beer and watched more holovid sports than I did in college," Bryce replied. "How's it feel to be law-abiding citizens again?"

Carl chuckled. "You mean how's it feel having everyone else think we are?" he asked. "I'll let you know once we've had a chance to land someplace where they care."

"Fair enough," Bryce replied. "I assume I'm good for the same bunk? Can't wait to see what you've done with the place."

Tanny set aside the installation instructions for their new holo-projector, and shadowed Bryce as he sauntered off down the corridor to the front of the ship. She wanted to be there when he saw.

He opened the door and stopped short. "You gotta be shitting me."

Tanny slouched against the wall beside him and crossed her arms. "Just the way you left it." Despite ample time, the *Mobius* was still on a ramen-dinner budget when it came to luxury purchases, and that included upgrades to the guest accommodations. Their remaining funds had gone into restocking the fridge and pantry, patching up the *Mobius* to Roddy's satisfaction, and picking up a stolen holo-projector at a steep discount.

Bryce let the footlocker dangle from his limp arm, dragging it on the floor as he trudged into his quarters. It must have been a shock going from the Rucker Resort's classy three-star decor with wall-to-wall holovids and all the gambling you could stomach, to the bare walls and cot of the *Mobius*.

The controls of the *Mobius* felt good in Tanny's hands. The grips on the flight yoke were worn where her hands always rested, the seat cushion padding crushed into the shape of her buttocks and lower back. The subtle hum that vibrated throughout every surface when the engines were running was back, and that was a comfort all its own. The worst of the waiting was over. It was mission time.

How Carl had gotten Janice to go along with the plan, she didn't know. Mort probably knew. Roddy would have wheedled the details out of him. But when Carl had returned from the Rucker Resort grinning like a bandit, she had given him such a glare that he had kept his methods to himself. He had managed to keep his mouth shut about it even from the co-pilot's seat, where he monitored the comm and sensors.

Formation flying wasn't something Tanny had done much in recent years. It was like being back in the marines, in the cockpit of a drop ship. The controls were different. There were fewer crude comments from grunts racked up in the drop bay. But the low-intensity thinking of just following the other ships and waiting for updated orders was the same as ever.

"If this thing goes sideways, Mort's ready to drop us out of the convoy's astral depth," Carl mentioned. He just couldn't sit there keeping his mouth shut. It was downright psychiatric. Mort was *always* ready to try something stupid and dangerous to flex his magical muscle. She ignored him and hoped he would take the hint.

They were still in Poet-controlled space, using the fleet's astral gate out to the edge of the Freeride System. Twelve mining ships, including the large, clumsy colony ship, drifted along amid their escort. Janice's *Alley Cat*, a Shadow class blockade running, led the way. The *Mobius* took the port side of the formation, with the *Atlantis Dream*—a militia patrol craft under Bill's command—on the starboard. Taking up the rear was a temporary escort from the Poet Fleet, a pair of light cruisers that could dust the lot of them, the *Do Rhetorical Questions Require Punctuation* and the *It Tolls For Thee*.

It was only minutes to the astral gate that would take them back to real space at the outskirts of Freeride. Once they dropped out of the public astral space, the convoy would engage their own star-drives and head out of system. Tanny keyed the comm to the engine room. "Roddy, all systems check out?"

"No, that new holo-projector is a piece of junk," Roddy came back through the cockpit speakers.

Carl leaned across to Tanny's side of the cockpit. "Hey, it was the best we were getting in Carousel. You rather be stuck watching me and Mort play Battle Minions?"

"The *ship's* system, Roddy," Tanny said. "Engines, shields ... the stuff that matter *now*."

"Engines are 4 percent under ideal efficiency, probably due to fuel impurities, but it could be a misalignment in the ignition subsystem. Shields are iffy; the dissipation coefficient is only 29 percent, but it's not like we can power them up any higher than 30 or 35 with the engines and guns on line. Life support reports a pressure increase over nominal in the waste reclaim, and I'm pretty sure with Kubu around, that's going to need regular maintenance. Internal power distribution—"

"She just wants the military version," Carl said.

Roddy's snort carried clearly through the comm. "Okie dokie, cap'n. We're good as gum for a gunfight."

Tanny gave Carl a withering look, but he just smirked back with a silent laugh in his eyes. How could he keep the jester act when they were about to engage in a mission? Even with the Recitol telling her that worrying was for weaklings, she could feel her palms sweating.

"*Roy, Barnum & Toyoda Mining Expedition fleet, you are cleared for astral exit,*" Captain Jan Toivonen, commander of the *It Tolls For Thee*, said.

"*Roger that,*" came the reply from Commander Bilkken of the mining convoy. "*Thanks for the escort.*"

Carl shook his head. "They actually sound grateful."

"They're Sol based," Tanny said. "They're probably pissing themselves being this far from an ARGO battle group. There's no Vendetta class interceptor cruisers to bail them out if they get in trouble. Those pirates probably looked like real protection to them."

"You're not getting cold feet, are you?" Carl asked.

"No," Tanny lied. This was all worked out and finalized. If they wanted their records to stay cleared, Esper back, and no one sentenced to decades of prison time, they had to follow through. "I just... they're like lambs to the slaughter."

"No slaughter," Carl replied. "I got Janice to buy off on that. We fuck this up in a 'prosecutor and judge' sorta way, it'll be simple piracy, not murder."

"What's that?"

"In years?" Carl asked. Tanny nodded. Carl was the one who normally worried about that end of things. "Fifteen for you guys, twenty for me as the ship's owner. That's if the big boys get us. If we got rounded up by local militias or someone besides an ARGO species, they'd probably dust us without hailing."

"I swore we'd never stoop to this," Tanny muttered. They'd done a lot of low jobs: theft, smuggling, illegal salvage. But this was the first time they'd ever attacked another ship preemptively.

Carl turned a shrug into an elaborate stretch, then laced his fingers behind his neck. "We've sworn lots of things, you and me. I've sworn to tell the truth, the whole truth, and nothing but. You've sworn to love, honor, and cherish. This shit slides."

You want, I can have Roddy draw up some fake divorce papers to get you out of swearing never to become a pirate."

"Give it a rest." It was different, and Carl had to have known it was different. The fact that he could make one thing sound like another was part of the way he helped them on jobs. But Tanny was going to be damned if she was going to let him sit there and twist her around until she agreed with him. He was taking advantage of her tenuous mental state.

"I'm just saying, if it's the promise that's bothering you, we can—"

Her fist acted on reflex. She was already feeling the sting in her knuckles before she realized she'd done it. Carl fell across the console on the far side of the co-pilot's chair. He stumbled out of his seat, clutching a hand to his mouth. The sounds coming out were undoubtedly vulgar, but they were equally incomprehensible.

"I'm sorry, I—"

Carl ignored her and staggered down the corridor to the rest of the ship.

Tanny hadn't intended to hit him. She had just wanted him to shut up, or at least change the subject. He had been asking for it. She had warned him. It was *his* fault, really. Hadn't he known her long enough to realize that she was liable to haul off and hit him if he pushed her too far? Too far was just closer than usual these days. She had mellowed herself out by experimenting with mood-levelers over the years. But she'd had a quick trigger when they first met. He ought to have remembered.

"Oh God," Tanny muttered, alone in the cockpit. "Am I going back to what I was like when I mustered out?" Back in those days, she had no friends. Her marine buddies had stayed in the service or taken the free detox. Old acquaintances shunned her, afraid of how much she'd changed, and she didn't let new people close. Carl had put up with her out of an odd mixture of thrill seeking, a shared interest in drinking, and—if she was honest with herself—the fact that she was raging with suppressed hormonal needs that he positioned himself to benefit from.

"*This is* Alley Cat, *check in prior to astral drop,*" Janice's voice from the comm startled Tanny.

"Alley Cat, *this is* Atlantis Dream. *Ready to dive,*" Bill replied.

Tanny fumbled for the button to open the comm. "This is *Mobius.* We'll follow you in."

Switching to ship-wide comm, she continued. "Mort, when you feel the convoy drop, bring us with them."

Kubu watched Mort. When Mommy talked from the wall, she told him to drop them. Kubu wasn't sure he liked that, but it being dropped was probably better than being locked up in Mommy's room. Mommy's room was small and boring, and she didn't listen to him when he told her so. But he was only a good boy if he stayed and didn't chew on anything, so he stayed, and didn't chew on anything. Mort had said it was OK to come out, and had opened the door.

Mort danced and sang, but his words were silly and didn't make any sense. The words didn't hurt, but they made Kubu's ears feel funny. When Mort was finished his dancing song, he sat down on the couch. Kubu jumped up beside him.

"That was funny," Kubu said, opening his mouth in a wide smile with his tongue hanging loose.

Mort frowned. "Funny, eh? The flarngmoot ziffod of the gipgop is funny to you?" Mort used more silly words than anyone.

Kubu nodded. "You say funny words. Thank you for letting Kubu out."

"Well, it's Bryce's turn to get locked in a room, at least until we're done with this job," Mort said.

Kubu cocked his head. "Who is Bryce? Does someone else have two names, like Mommy?"

Mort laughed through his nose. "No. You remember Bryce. He was here before we landed. You scared him, so Tanny made you stay in the room."

Kubu's eyes went wide. "The bad man is back?"

Mort rubbed a rough hand on Kubu's head. "Oh, he's harmless."

"No," Kubu replied. "He wants to put us in cages. Mommy's friend in the wall said so."

"That's actually Tanny talking over the ship's comm," Mort said. "You get used to it."

"No, not *now*," Kubu said. "Before. Mommy's friend was talking from the wall, and the bad man is playing a trick to put us in cages."

Mort grabbed Kubu under the chin and looked him right in the eyes. The mustard on his breath made Kubu's tummy jealous and grumbly. "Esper called you?"

Kubu nodded. "Esper is Mommy's friend. She made the wall talk, just like Mommy does."

"Gadzooks! Esper sent us a warning," Mort said. "Why didn't you say anything sooner?"

Kubu hung his head. It seemed he hadn't been such a good boy after all. "Bad man was gone."

Mort jumped up from the couch and ran to Mommy's flying room.

Mort burst into the cockpit. "We've got a problem!"

Seated at the controls, Tanny would have leapt out of her seat if she wasn't buckled in. "God dammit, Mort! Get out of here!"

Mort waved away her concerns. "No time for that," Mort said. "That Bryce fellow is a plant."

"This is not time to get metaphysical," Tanny said. "Keep it together."

"You're not listening clearly," Mort replied. "Bryce isn't flora, he's a double agent. Think *The Three-Sided Coin* or *The Julian Affair*, except this time it's not on the holo and it's *our* keesters in the cross-hairs."

Tanny lifted her arms to an uncaring universe. "You just came to this revelation... how?"

"Kubu—"

"Good Lord, Mort! He's got the intelligence of an infant. You can't be taking him seriously."

"Esper left a message," Mort said. "Must have been while we were over at the resort. 'Bad man tricking us, wants to put us in cages.' Sound like something Esper might try to simplify to Kubuian comprehension."

"Shit." Mort was right. If any of them were going to trust a barely sentient dog with their lives, it would be Esper—though she wouldn't put it past Carl, either.

"Shit, indeed," Mort agreed.

Tanny keyed the comm to the engine room. "Roddy, get up here and fly this thing."

Mort furrowed his brow. "Doesn't Mriy usually take care of that?"

It was true, Mriy was their backup pilot, but that was almost by default. Roddy was needed elsewhere, whereas Mriy was dead weight in the Black Ocean if she didn't help mind the cockpit. But this time, it was Roddy whose skills could be spared. Tanny's thoughts were a blur, but there was one thing that was certain: they needed help, and it wasn't help they were going to find on board.

"Not this time," Tanny said.

As the door to her quarters slammed shut, Tanny allowed her frustration to show. She punched her mattress once, then again, then kept on punching it until her breath came in gasps. How could they have been so stupid? How could they have left the background check to Carl's "keen" eye? They needed to find out who Bryce Brisson really was, who he worked for, and some way that they might get some leverage to pry themselves out of the jam he had put them in. Tanny needed that background check, and someone who could do it *right*.

The datapad was the heaviest hundred grams she could have imagined. It took an act of will to lift it from her bedside and key in a code she had known since childhood, one she had to memorize, one she was only supposed to use in an emergency.

A cheery little waiting indicator swirled on the screen, informing Tanny that though nothing appeared to be happening, the datapad was hard at work in the background. They were a long ways from the Sol System, and the deepest, fastest astral omni relays were the most likely to be tapped by intelligence and law enforcement agencies. Even at nearly the speed of light, signals took time to travel at just four astral units deep.

"Hello?" a deep, puzzled voice asked. It was as familiar as her old bedroom, a voice filled with bedtime stories and promises of ice cream and ponies. Tanny's throat tightened.

"Hello? Who is this? How's you get this ID? This comm is over—"

"Daddy, wait!" Tanny blurted.

"Tania? Is that you?" her father asked.

"Daddy, I've got a problem," Tanny said.

"You know you can—"

"I got caught up in something," Tanny continued. "I trusted someone I shouldn't have, and it looks like we're going to end up getting caught up with Janice and her crew in a blue-hat trap. But my info might be wrong, and if it's wrong, I could sour a huge job, and maybe get some poor slob killed over nothing. We just didn't have the kind of resources to find out ahead of time whether—"

"Sweety, calm down," her father said. "I musta told you a hundred times; I don't care what you've done. I'll always be there for you. What do you need?"

Tanny sniffed. She wiped her eyes. "We picked up a guy," she said, clearing her throat. "Alias is Bryce Brisson. We did a background check, but nothing flagged as dangerous. Small-time data hustler; he did a little time. But we got a tip from someone being held by the Poet Fleet that this guy might be a mole. Can you dig him up good? Find out who he really is?"

"Sure, Tania," her father said. "Gimme an hour—two tops."

"Can you manage fifteen minutes?"

"You're that pinched?" her father asked.

"I'd try for five if I thought it was even possible."

"Hold on." The datapad went silent for a moment. "I got a guy on it. He knows this is important to me."

"Thank you, Daddy."

"Just one thing," her father said. "Can we put this on video comm? Just for a minute... please?"

Tanny closed her eyes and took a slow breath. She turned on the camera feed from her datapad. Don Rucker appeared on her screen, just as she would be appearing on his. He looked older. The last time she had seen him had been over a grudging invitation to her third wedding, but he'd been dressed to the nines and professionally styled. Now, his hair showed more gray than black, and the wrinkles around his mouth had deepened. But when he saw her, the familiar smile she had always remembered came back.

"There's my little girl," he said. A twinkle of mischief appeared in his eye. "You look like hell, though. Carl not taking good care of you?"

"I take care of myself, Daddy," Tanny replied. "And I'm just getting older, same as you. You look a little like hell, yourself."

"Maybe you oughtta finally quit that shit the marines got you hooked on," her father said. "If it's money, I can pay for the nicest place you'd ever want to dry out."

"It's not the money," Tanny replied. "That shit costs more than detox would. It's just who I am now. Even Carl accepts that now, more or less."

"Well, maybe Carl just don't love you like I do," her father said. "My offer stands. You ever find yourself changing your mind, don't let money stop you. There's a place on the other side of Mars; they'd take good care of you."

"Let me know as soon as your guy runs his check," Tanny replied, shifting the topic back to the identity of Bryce Brisson.

"You got it, sweety," her father said. "It was good to hear from you, whatever the reason."

Tanny closed the comm. She wiped her eyes in earnest, and they welled up again in an instant. Dammit, she needed Sepromax! If she were herself, she never would have called her father for help. She certainly wouldn't have broken down crying like a five-year-old afterward. Thoughts of reporting back to the crew about the outcome of her call were abandoned, and Tanny let herself cry until the tears ran dry.

Bryce Brisson slammed into the wall, his toes just barely touching the floor. Mriy's grip around his throat was just loose enough for him to breathe. He tried to push the azrin away, but her arms were a quarter meter longer; he couldn't so much as reach her chest or face. Instead, he settled for grabbing onto the corded muscle of her forearm to support himself.

"It's all clear," Mriy called out. The rest of the crew filed into the converted conference room that Bryce had been given as quarters.

Tanny felt wrung out. Her eyes were still red in the mirror, but she was past the crying. When her father had called back, their brief exchange had been (almost) all business. Anger had prevented her from breaking down again, and her father's demeanor had reminded her why they hadn't patched things up between them. Don Rucker was one ruthless son-of-a-bitch, and it came across the omni loud and clear.

"Carl, Mort, one of you talk some sense into this crazy xeno," Bryce said.

"Trust me," Carl said, slipping inside and slouching against the wall by the door. He was still holding a hand to his sore jaw. "Mriy's the reasonable one here. Tanny would have broken both your legs if it weren't for Mriy handling you."

Mriy extended a claw on her free hand with a flick, gesturing to the floor. A broken stun blaster lay amid shattered pieces of its outer casing. "I got blasted twice in my broken ribs."

"If you'd let the doctors see you, they wouldn't still be broken," Carl replied.

Tanny approached within arm's reach of Bryce. If the snake wanted to take a swing at her, she'd have been more than happy to rupture his spleen in return. "Let's cut to the chase. "Your name is Martin David Morse, age thirty-eight, from Stockholm Prime. You are a captain in the Earth Interstellar Enhanced Investigative Org."

"Someone set me up," Bryce insisted, struggling for air.

Tanny shook her head. "No, they didn't. *You* set *us* up. Someone put a lot of effort into burying the link between Martin Morse and Bryce Brisson. But not enough."

Carl rubbed his forehead between thumb and forefinger. "Marty-boy, you've put us in a delicate situation. We vouched for you, and your bullshit backstory fooled everyone up until now. Janice still believes you. But we're bait in a trap now, thanks to you and your cronies. By all rights, we should dust you right now."

"We kill a member of the constabulary, we can kiss that records purge goodbye," Mort said, more or less just as they'd rehearsed in the common room minutes ago. "It's clever, really. I bet if he doesn't come back, those records mysteriously get put back the way they were."

Bryce managed a spasmodic nod. "Guaranteed."

"Of course," Carl said, sounding philosophical. "There's nothing that says they won't get restored even after this is over. That is, even if we don't get netted by lawmen before then. You've fucked us good."

"Simplest solution," said Mriy. "Kill him. Run."

Carl wagged a finger. "Don't be hasty. We still might come out of this with a clean rap sheet and our hides if we play this right. Everyone just give me a quiet minute to think this out."

Tanny glared holes in Bryce. Martian authorities had been trying for generations to bring her family down. They'd had their victories here and there. Plenty of her family had done time for one crime or another, and they had spent a fortune on lawyers over the years. As much as she'd have enjoyed breaking Bryce's neck herself, lawyers were the way to deal with EIEIO, and Carl was the closest they had on board.

Carl snapped his fingers. "I got it. Try this one on for size. You make a call, get your friends to drop their ambush, and we let you go once the hijacking is over."

Bryce managed a quick shake of his head. "They'd know something was up. The Ruckers would get arrested as planned, and you'd end up killing me."

"Jesus, Carl," Tanny said. "Weaseling out of our fuck-ups is supposed to be your specialty. Roddy could have come up with that plan."

Carl's eyebrows leapt. "Ooh, I've got a better one. This solves *our* problem, too. We don't jack the ships to sell them, Janice takes them and settles a new headquarters with that colony ship and gets herself a little fleet of cargo ships, maybe sells off some of the mining gear and cuts us in."

"Uh, Carl," Mort said, standing in the doorway. "That still leaves us walking into a trap."

Carl began to pace. Tanny had seen him do it enough to know that it meant he was stumped. Carl didn't like pacing— probably didn't even realize he was doing it. "How are they going to intercept the fleet? Up until Janice orders the attack, it's just freelance work."

"We could just escort them to Platt, take their money, and worry how to get Esper free after," Tanny suggested.

Mort shook his head. "The Poets aren't the fools those Sol lawmen are. I'd rather deal with them and dupe Martin's buddies."

"You can call me Bryce, still."

Mriy snarled in his face. "No one asked you."

"I almost hate to bring this up," Tanny said. "But he wasn't lying when he told Janice he was a family man."

Bryce's eyes went wide, and he struggled in Mriy's grasp. "You wouldn't!"

Carl frowned. "I'm inclined to agree with him."

"Let's just put it this way," Tanny said. "My father knows what's going on out here. Half of Janice's crew is blood relatives, even if a few are a couple generations sideways of the main family line. You think he's going to just let this slide if Janice goes down? We won't have to do shit."

Carl folded his arms and leaned against the wall. "Don just seems like such a good guy, though..." A slow grin spread across his face.

Tanny gave a nod and Mriy dropped Bryce, who fell to his hands and knees. "Well, Bryce, looks like we're all in the shit one way or another. Your cover is blown to hell. You're as good as dusted, and I wouldn't want to be Trisha, Benjamin, or Todd right now." Naming his wife and boys seemed just enough to set Bryce into a full-on panic.

"You can't let him do anything to them," Bryce pleaded. "I'm doing my job out here, busting my ass to make the galaxy a little safer for them and everyone else. But they haven't done anything. They don't even know where I am for months on end. You've gotta explain that to your father."

"We've never seen eye to eye on how to handle family business," Tanny said. "Plus, why would I bail you out while we're still caught up on the cliff's edge?"

"Maybe we should kill him," Mort suggested.

"Mort talks sense," Mriy agreed.

"—same way we killed Esper."

"Wait? What?" Bryce spluttered, from the floor.

"OK," Tanny said. "This is going somewhere."

"You killed Esper?" Bryce asked.

Carl walked around and stood over Bryce as the double-agent squirmed into a seated position on the floor. "We faked it. I suppose we could fake it for you, too."

"How's that help us, though?" Tanny asked. That might spare Bryce the complications that fell out of the plan, for better or worse, but she couldn't see how it benefited any of them. If only she was balanced out; the right mix of brain chemicals would smooth out her jumbled thoughts until these connections made sense.

"He can help us," Carl said. "No, I've got this worked out. He calls in a last-minute update for whoever the hell is coming after us. New coordinates. Operational security meant that we altered the convoy's course so we couldn't be intercepted. Martin here sends them the updated course."

"But we go on the original course?" Bryce asked, a note of hope in his voice.

"No!" Carl shouted with a grin. He held up a finger to the ceiling. "We *do* change the course, but not to the one we feed you."

"Sounds like it could work," Tanny said, impressed. "But how do we convince Janice?"

Carl cracked his knuckles. "That'll be the easiest part. Leave it to me."

❁ ❁ ❁

Alone in the astral gray. Or at least, as alone as fifteen ships can be. Traveling 2.5 astral units deep would earn a captain a hefty fine from any patrol vessel, but it was unlikely that anyone was going to stumble across the ships of Operation RIBBIT. The non-standard depth was just another precaution against someone taking a casual interest in their passing, but if Commander Bilkken of the mining convoy knew anything about fringe space, he would have known that the half depths were the highways of the undesirables.

"*Convoy, full stop,*" Janice ordered over the comm. "*Prepare to receive next-leg coordinates. Also, we have a maintenance issue on the* Mobius. *Please stand by to dock for a quick repair. We'll be underway in twenty minutes.*" This was it. Carl had been scant on the details, but his revised plan had the *Mobius* crew boarding the colony ship and spearheading the hijacking.

"Alley Cat," Commander Bilkken replied. "*Is this repair urgent? We're only two days out from Platt.*"

"*Affirmative,*" Janice replied. "*It's an engine mis-ajustment that's going to leave a heavy ion trail if we don't get it corrected. Anyone tries to track our course change, they'd be able to follow it.*"

"*Very well, Alley Cat,*" Commander Bilkken replied. "*Just be quick about it. I don't like sitting idle in astral space.*"

"Sissy," Tanny muttered. "We do it all the time."

Carl stood at the back of the cockpit, still nursing a sore jaw. "Yeah, but half the shit we do in the astral oughtta get us killed, so I don't know that it's bravery so much as desensitization. We're just too stupid to be scared of off-the-standards depths. Mort ever keels while we're down deep, we're just fucked."

Roddy slipped into the cockpit past Carl and stood on the co-pilot's seat. He pointed at Tanny and hooked a thumb toward the back of the ship. "Beat it, knuckles. I'm flying us into their hangar."

Tanny turned to Carl, ignoring the laaku. "What?"

Carl jerked his head, motioning for her to follow as he backed out of the cockpit. "Come on. You're not ready to be part of *this* little boarding party yet. Not dressed like that."

"What's wrong with how I'm dressed?" Tanny demanded. She was already in her ablative armor with a sidearm strapped at either thigh. Grab a helmet and blaster rifle on the way out and she was good to invade.

But Carl didn't answer. It was both a welcome change of pace for him, but the mischievous grin made it ominous all the same.

The three of them stood on the cargo ramp, ready to be lowered down as the ramp opened. Tanny felt ridiculous. Mort had magicked up a strapless red cocktail dress and a bowler hat with an ostrich feather stuck in the brim like an inkpot. If she hadn't been holding a blaster rifle, Carl would be snickering at her, and she couldn't have blamed him.

Not that Carl looked any less ludicrous in a black-and-white checkerboard suit and cowboy hat. To accessorize his costume, he carried his glyphed sword (which he had no business using in a fight), disguised to look like a gentleman's cane, and—of all things—a monocle. Where he had gotten the huge cigar he chomped down on as he waited, Tanny didn't know, but it wasn't a figment of Mort's magic. It would have taken special software to recognize him; Tanny's features were only disguised by a hooker's share of makeup, magically applied.

She didn't know if Mriy had gotten off easy, or if her disguise was the most humiliating of the bunch. She wore her usual vest with the high, hard back that protected her neck, and a worn pair of loose red slacks. But her fur was now a psychedelic swirl of colors, most of which didn't belong on a sentient creature. There was a striped pattern that peeked meekly from the chaos, reminiscent of a Bengal tiger's markings.

It was Carl's idea. It always seemed to be Carl's idea when things took a turn for the juvenile or self-abasing. Credit where credit was due, though: she barely recognized either of them.

Gas hissed as the atmospheric seal around the cargo ramp released. "Places, everyone," Carl sang, already in character. Tanny shifted her blaster rifle out of easy view as the ramp lowered.

A small team of personnel in drab gray coveralls were waiting for them. One held a datapad; the others carried standard issue tool and diagnostic kits. The apparent leader consulted his datapad. "Some sort of E-M leakage? We'll see what we can—"

"Nobody move!" Tanny shouted. She whipped her blaster rifle from behind her and aimed it at the one with the datapad. Without pausing for the mechanics to overcome their shock, she marched down the ramp, the red dot from her rifle's laser sight holding a steady position on the mechanic's sternum. Say one thing for the Recitol, it gave her fluid muscle control and balance.

One of the other two mechanics flinched. Maybe he was just nervous. Maybe he was reaching for a comm. But Mriy caught the man's hand as it reached for a pocket. With a twist and one of Tanny's takedown techniques, the mechanic was facedown on the floor in two seconds, with Mriy's boot on the back of his neck.

"That was moving," Carl pointed out cheerfully. He pointed to the remaining mechanic, stiff with fright. "See? He's got it right. Now if you'll excuse us, we're taking your ship. If you play nice, you'll be home safe and snug in a few days." He paused a moment and looked around the ship's hangar. "Unless you live on this tub, in which case you're being evicted."

Roddy scrambled down the ramp as soon as all the mechanics were rounded up with their hands bound behind their backs. He carried a plasma torch and a scan-all, with his own coveralls stuffed with smaller tools. "Give me three minutes."

"Comm first, then main power," Carl reminded him.

"You fucking idi—knave," Roddy shouted over his shoulder, correcting himself at the last second. He wasn't in costume, but there was still some degree of character to maintain. "I know my job."

Mort ambled down the ramp. "Am I my brother's keeper? Would that I could find one to become that brother?" he asked rhetorically. Mort, for one, had an ear for the archaic.

Tanny checked her wrist chrono. Two and a half more minutes for Roddy to bring down the colony ship's communications, then it would be time to play pirate. Three mechanics didn't count.

❀ ❀ ❀

Tanny blew the reinforced door to the bridge off its hinges with a pair of Galex-B charges Janice had provided. That much, at least, had been in the original plan. The rest was new, and Carl's last-minute addition of a costumed frame-job was still being modified as they made their way through the corridors of the nameless colony ship, designation Roy Barnum Toyoda 001.

"Who do you think you are?" Commander Bilkken demanded. The commander of the mining convoy wasn't a fancy naval captain, but he had a crispness about his person, from his close-trimmed hair to his wrinkle-free uniform. He looked from Tanny in her nightclub costume ball getup to Mriy, painted like a tiger gone kaleidoscopic.

Of course, Carl wouldn't let attention linger anywhere but on him. "Some people call me the space cowboy," Carl said. Tanny furrowed her brow. "Some call me the gangster of love." He turned and winked his non-monocle eye at the ship's navigator, a woman with dark, tightly curled hair who shied away and looked at her console. "But you can call me Maurice."

"What is the meaning of this?" Commander Bilkken demanded. Tanny was impressed. For a guy without so much as a drawn sidearm, he was talking a good game. "We contracted with Janice Rucker for safe passage to Platt."

Carl gestured flamboyantly with his cane and the datapad he held in his other hand. "Ah, you contracted with Janice Rucker, but there's the rub. We don't work for her. Ships can wear false faces as easily as men. And ours are false indeed. You see, when you left Freeride, you thought you were escorted by two ships of the Poet Fleet, who said their 'fare you well' and 'God keep you.' But what if it were five, and but two parted ways with a wink and a share of mischief."

Carl whirled, datapad at arm's length. While Commander Bilkken was shielded from view of the screen, Carl took a quick glance, checking his cribbed notes.

"I got a guarantee from Admiral Chisholm herself that we would get safe passage through Freeride," Commander Bilkken snarled. "She..." Some realization seemed to dawn on the commander just then.

"We're not *in* Freeride, Commander Bilkken," Carl pointed out. "Words can mean very particular and precise things, and I should thank you to take better care with them in the future."

"What's your game, Maurice?" Commander Bilkken asked.

"This and this alone: a profit," Carl said. He twirled the cane in his hand, and Tanny winced, wondering whether he was going to forget it was a sword and cut off his own fingers. "But we wish no harm to you or your crew. If you would recall your crews and all pile aboard a single of the smaller vessels, we'll send you along to Platt without further delay."

"You're trifling with dangerous men, Mr. Maurice," Commander Bilkken said, lowering his voice to a threatening growl. "Misters Roy, Barnum, and Toyoda aren't men to rob."

Carl grinned and sidled up to Commander Bilkken, wrapping his sword arm around him, but carefully keeping the datapad out of view. "My good commander, many would have said the same of the Rucker Syndicate. In fact, many *more* than have ever heard of misters Roy, Barnum, and Toyoda combined. And yet, we Poets have removed Janice Rucker from this transaction, stolen the names of her ships, and shoved your eyes under the wool. You are welcome to inform your employers and anyone else you like of our part in this affair, once you're rescued. It would, in point of fact, greatly enhance our reputation. As Publilius Syrus once said, 'A good reputation is more valuable than money.'"

"Enough chatter, boss," Tanny said. Who knew how much thicker Carl was going to lay it on, or how many hollow platitudes he had loaded into that datapad? She wasn't going to wait for him to dig himself a hole deep enough for a grave. "Let's get these philistines onto a cargo ship and get out of here."

Carl gave a dramatic sigh and disentangled himself from Commander Bilkken. "If you would all be so good as to line up single file and not make any sudden movements, we can have you locked on autopilot to Platt by dinnertime."

Dozens of booted feet clomped down the steel hallway of the colony ship. Tanny had been assigned to herd the hijacked crew toward the docking port. Part of her dared any of them to make a sudden movement. These weren't smugglers, pirates, or military personnel, though, just spacers making a freight run in a bad neighborhood. They were probably scared *before* getting boarded.

Bilkken looked over his shoulder at Tanny as he walked at the back of the herd. "You're making a huge mistake."

"Keep it moving." Tanny jabbed him in the back with the muzzle of her rifle. She made a mental note to clean the weapon later; the commander's uniform was drenched in sweat.

But Bilkken kept talking, even as he faced forward. "You seem like the brains of this operation. Tell me what's really going on here. I had personal assurances from Admiral Chisholm that we'd have no troubles."

"Hey, we're doing you a favor. The Rucker Syndicate was going to dust the lot of you. Now, you just get a short vacation."

Bilkken hung his head. "I should have known something was up when Kristov got arrested planetside."

Curiosity peeked through the dull haze of chemicals. "Kristov?"

"My security chief. I knew that charge was bogus. I *knew* it! Kristov wasn't the sort to start fistfights. So some lowlife made a grab at her... she's handled that crap before..."

"Wait, your security chief—?"

When Bilkken turned, his furrowed brow showed genuine puzzlement. "You really are low down the flagpole, aren't you? You didn't know Chisholm had my security chief? Sprang her from lockup and kept her as a 'guest' on her flagship. Said we could swing by and pick her up on our way back after the delivery. None of this is deja vu?" He shook his head.

Pieces were falling into place. Esper had been set up. The run-in that resulted in her murder change was probably conceived as a simple assault. Chisholm had the whole system rigged, top to bottom. "Just what's the admiral supposedly do with these hostages? I only signed on a couple weeks back; this shit's all news to me."

He looked Tanny up and down. "Let's just say you and me aren't Chisholm's type. She likes 'em young and soft, from what I hear."

"But your security chief..."

"Kristov runs an explosive scanner and sweeps for trackers. She's a computer jockey, and since my wife's not here, I don't mind telling you she's a damn well-shaped one."

Tanny's mind raced. What was Esper caught up in? "What would she do to someone who rejected her advances?"

Bilkken chuckled, prompting Tanny to prod him with the rifle again. "Don't worry. Like I said, you're not her type. But if you're looking to grunt and sweat your way up the ranks, I'd lay off the gene splice and stims—whatever the hell you're on."

A few heads near the front of the crowd had turned to listen to their conversation. Tanny fired a shot into the ceiling over their heads. "Eyes forward."

"You don't sound like them... yet. Get out while you still can. That lifestyle just eats at your soul. Sex and wine. Theater and extortion. Easy living picking on the bones of someone else's hard work. It's like a drug."

He had a point about the lifestyle, but everyone had their drug. Maybe the Poets were helpless in the face of their own hedonism, but that was just their hangup. Mort had his magic. Carl couldn't help gambling. Roddy's alcoholism was painfully obvious. Esper was addicted to sticking her nose in other people's business. If Tanny's drug was literal, then so be it. The fact that she could acknowledge it meant that she had control, and the fact she noticed told her that the Sepromax was starting to kick in. This was Tanny thinking, not some chemical imbalance.

She had to give Bilkken credit, though. His ploy was a classic Psy Ops tactic. He had found a difference between her and the Poets and was driving a wedge into it as best he could. Too bad she wasn't really a neophyte pirate, or he might have had some luck.

"Well, buddy, maybe some of us like the drug."

The starport on Carousel was only slightly busier than the remote landing field the *Mobius* had used on its first visit. It wasn't used much for passenger traffic, serving mainly as an intermodal station for supply freighters and terrestrial shipping vehicles. Commerce of the blue-collar sort was going on all around the crew as they stood waiting at the bottom of the ship's cargo ramp.

Bryce was taking things better than expected. He stood motionless, staring out at the horizon beyond the chain-fenced boundary of the starport. A speck appeared in the sky on the approach vector they were expecting. Bryce swallowed. "I don't suppose this is negotiable."

"Bryce old buddy," Carl said. "You bought yourself a better bargain than you were in for, given the shit you tried to pull. But even if I was the fucking pope, I wouldn't be forgiving you like nothing happened."

"Suppose not," Bryce mumbled, then resumed his mute vigil.

It wasn't long before the speck grew large enough to be recognized as a spacecraft. Sleek, black, with lines like a racer and pristine as a showpiece, the ship landed fifty meters from the *Mobius*, sending up a wash of dust that had everyone but Bryce shielding their eyes.

Carl strode across to greet the new arrival. A side door opened, appeared from what had looked like a seamless panel of the sleek ship's hull, and two men exited. He clapped one on the back in a quick hug, and shook hands with the other. By the shake of their shoulders, Carl made both of them laugh.

"Which ones are they?" Bryce asked over his shoulder.

"My uncle Earl," Tanny said, deadpan. "And his son Jimmy."

"Earl Rucker..." Bryce repeated. His fists tightened at his side.

"If you're thinking of running... " Tanny warned.

Bryce shook his head. "I got your word. I go quiet, and you make sure your father leaves my family alone."

"This our vermin?" Earl asked in a bass voice as he approached. "Don't look like much." Earl was a wall, with shoulders nearly as wide as he was tall, and a neck like a tree trunk.

"Ain't that the point, pop?" Jimmy asked. Though smaller than his father, Jimmy was larger than the bouncers at most rough nightclubs.

"So this gray fuzz-top tried pinning that Lorstram hit on you guys?" Earl asked, poking Bryce in the chest with a hot-dog-sized finger.

Bryce cringed slightly. "Yeah," he replied, voice dry.

Jimmy laughed, and Earl chuckled along. Jimmy jostled Bryce with a forearm. "Lighten up, pigeon. We ain't sore winners. You got luckier than you even know, blowin' this job."

"Come on," Earl said, pinching Bryce by the cheek like an adoring aunt. "We'll take good care of you, long as you keep your yap shut and play nice."

They exchanged good-byes. The Ruckers remembered Roddy by name, but not Mriy. The two behemoths shook hands with Mort, but looked as if they were grabbing a blaster by the wrong end in doing so. Never had either of the two looked less intimidating. There were hugs for Tanny and handshakes for Carl, along with the ever-open offer to come work with them.

"Maybe next time," Carl said with a wink before they took Bryce and returned to their ship.

The sleek, black craft slid back into space like a sliver of night, disappearing into the darkness.

The crew of the *Mobius* went back inside and killed another two hours watching local system news on the holovid until it was time to reconvene. The sun was low in the sky when the sheriff's department shuttle touched down within meters of where the Rucker ship had landed. It was mere seconds before the ship's door opened and someone stepped out. It took longer for Tanny to realize it was Esper. She was wearing an ankle-length black dress and heeled leather boots, with an ermine stole wrapped around her neck against the cold. A sheriff's deputy followed her out, dragging a trunk with its own repulsors.

Esper waved a gloved hand and ran across the patch of dusty tarmac between the ships. Tanny had a sly curiosity as to who she'd seek out first. She'd an impression for a while now—two in fact—that both Carl and Mort had more than a passing interest in her well-being. Carl she understood. Esper's brain-fried mother had gotten her surgically sculpted into one of those dolls designed by mammary-obsessed creeps. The girl was practically designed to make drooling idiots like Carl into bigger drooling idiots. Not her fault; not even his. But Mort generally kept above that, clinging to the estranged family he'd left on Earth. If he snuck some on the side, he'd kept it discreet. Yet he doted on Esper in a frankly unfatherly manner, taking her faith as more of a challenge than a roadblock. He was a wizard, but that didn't mean his self-control was iron.

As her run brought her closer, Tanny drew back in surprise. Esper was headed *her* way. They had gotten friendly, after all, but she had expected a couple weeks of captivity would have left Esper a little more ... pent up. But the impression passed quickly as Esper crouched low. Kubu separated himself from the crew and rushed forward the last few meters to meet her.

"Kubu, you did great!" Esper said. "You're a hero."

"Kubu is a hero?" Kubu asked. He licked Esper's face. "You are much nicer now that you're not a wall any more."

"I'm happy not to *be* a wall any more," Esper replied. She looked up to everyone else. "And thank you guys for believing him. I don't know how much longer I could have held out there."

"Yeah," Roddy said. "You're looking rough. Were the pedicures every *other* day, or every third?"

"Where should I put your trunk, Miss Richelieu?" the deputy asked.

"Just inside," Esper replied. "I'll unpack it myself." She seemed to realize the rest of the crew were staring at her. "What? They gave me clothes to wear. It's not like any of *them* are going to wear anything second-hand. Why let all those nice outfits go to waste?"

Carl scratched his head. "You *sure* you want to come back?"

Esper nodded vigorously. "It was like I was being hunted. It eventually got to the point where it felt like everyone on that ship was trying to sleep with me. It was Sodom, Gomorrah, and Vegas rolled into one."

"That's it," Carl said. "Next time, I'm getting captured by the pirates. You all can skip the rescue."

Mort snorted. "These pirates wouldn't have you. These are *educated* pirates."

"Sophisticated, even," Esper agreed.

"I could fake that," Carl said, sounding hurt.

"Yeah," Tanny said with a sigh. "He could."

Tanny sat on her bed, alone. Beside her was a digitally locked crate, given to her by Janice before they parted ways in the middle of astral nowhere. A gift, she had called it. Tanny would receive the combination to open it once Janice and her crew had gotten themselves to a suitable destination to drop the colony ship planetside. That had been four days ago. Tanny had been tempted to challenge Mort or Roddy to open it, as much to spite Janice as to discover the contents. If she knew Janice, it was going to be an insulting gift anyway. But every morning, she took the crate, set it on the bed, and kept it company as she waited for word from her cousin.

Today her vigil ended. She had set an alarm on her datapad for messages from Janice. It played a few bars of a heavy melody, filled with doom and dread. Janice had finally sent word:

To Tania,

We found a place that's half shithole and set ourselves up in the half that isn't. No offense, but you don't get to know where. I know we butted heads for a lot of years, but you at least know how to work a job. If that Bryce had found dumber patsies, I'd be in lock-up right about now, or maybe dead. So I owe you for that.

To make things up, the combination is in the attached file. Oh, and I didn't fuck Carl when he stayed over at the resort. I just got him to play along and let you think I did. It would have been weird. Carl's family, after all. Anyway, go ahead and open that crate. You earned it.

J.R.

Tanny opened the file appended to Janice's message, and fed the multi-layer encryption key into the crate. The lock popped with a soft puff of released pressure. Opening the lid, Tanny gasped.

Inside was everything she needed: Centrimac, Plexophan, Adrenophiline, Pseudoanorex, Zygrana, Cannabinol, and even Recitol. It had the mineral supplements she needed. There was even a supply of Sepromax. There was no way Janice could have gotten all that without Carl's help. Only the crew and a couple suppliers might have been able to pass that detailed mix along.

The song of doom played from Tanny's datapad once more, and there was another message:

I figure you got it open by now. Just so you know, that's your cut. If you want a profit on this job, sell that shit at the nearest hellhole for marine burnouts. But if you want to stay hooked on that shit, it's none of my business.

J.R.

An hour later, Tanny was beginning to feel like her *old* self again. Not her old old self, but the one she had been for most of her time serving on the *Mobius*. Things were starting to make sense again. She wasn't feeling as paranoid, unfocused, or inexplicably angry. She was feeling enough like herself to feel guilty about taking the crew's cut for herself, and but not enough that she was about to change her mind.

"I'll make it up to them," she told herself.

As far as offices went, Bryce Brisson had seen more impressive. He'd seen the section chief's office, with its so-new-they-sparkle holo consoles, polished glass desk and chairs, and oil portraits of Earth prime ministers and former section chiefs. He'd been to Oxford on an investigation once and seen a dean's office appointed with antiques that cost more than his annual salary. But those and others lacked one aspect that made this office more intimidating than all the others combined: it had Don Rucker sitting in it.

The syndicate boss looked just like the holos Bryce had seen for years working in Crime Disorganization. Take Don Rucker out of his expensive suit, confiscate his gold wrist-chrono, and remove him from his fawning associates, and you'd never tell him apart from a freight handler or a prison guard. He had the muscular shoulders of a man who once did his own leg breaking, and the ample gut of someone who'd had people for that sort of thing for a long while. But in the squareness of his jaw and the hard, disapproving glare, Bryce could see a lot of Tanny in him.

"So, this is the guy?" Don Rucker asked. It was a formality. Bryce knew the Rucker Syndicate had dug up everything they needed to undo him. There was no chance of mistaken identity.

"Sure is, Don," Earl replied. "He came nice and peaceful."

Don leaned back in his chair. "A man resigned to his fate?"

Bryce swallowed. He tried to say something, but no sound came. He licked his lips and tried again. "A man with everything to lose."

Don nodded with his lips pressed tight. "Yeah, you do. That wife of yours was a looker ten, fifteen years ago. I bet that's still the way you see her." He pressed a button on a console set into his desk. A tabletop holo popped up, showing Trisha walking down the street with an armload of groceries.

Bryce made a short, jittery twitch of his neck muscles meant to convey a nod.

"And those boys of yours..." Don let the holo finish his statement. With a press of another button, the holo changed, and it was Ben and Todd hopping onto the tram after school. They were heading home. Home. Bryce was never going to see home again. His lip quivered as he struggled to maintain his composure in front of the Ruckers.

"That's why you're standing here right now, isn't it?" Don asked, pointing less at Bryce and more toward the floor where he stood. "You coulda run. You coulda fought back. But you're just standing here—eyes welling up like your dog just died." Don hit a button and the holo disappeared.

"You've got me," Bryce said. "They don't know anything. They haven't done anything."

"Be a shame, seeing them scraping by on that ARGO widow's fund payout," Don said. The mention of his wife being a widow set the tears rolling down Bryce's face. "Oh, for the love of God. Jimmy, pour this guy a drink. What I was saying is that I don't see a reason she has to raise those boys on one salary and the chump change ARGO pays out for a killed-on-duty." Bryce felt a tumbler pressed into his hands and absently brought it to his mouth. The liquid burned from lips to throat, but he drank. He tipped it back, relishing the pain. He came up for air gasping, and doubled over. Someone took the glass when he offered it back.

Don, Earl, and Jimmy had a laugh at his expense. "Janice was right," Don said. "This one's not all bad. I tell you what, Mr. Undercover Tech Sneak; today's your lucky day. I've got an offer for you, and you'd be wise to take it."

Bryce put his hand on his knees and pushed himself mostly upright. "An offer?" he asked, his voice hoarse.

"I like having people with inside knowledge," Don said. "You're going to come work for me?"

Bryce shook his head. "I can't. I won't betray ARGO."

"ARGO? What have they done for you?" Don asked.

"Nothing," Earl added.

"They ship you off to the cold, dark side of the galaxy. No backup. No bonus pay. You risk your life so some silver-spoon lawyers don't get their ships boosted," Don said. "You work for me ... well, let's say it's a safer life, believe it or not. New name, new digs, maybe a little cosmo so they don't catch you on a biometric scan. Life gets a little harder for those boys who hung you out to dry in Freeride; life gets a little easier for Trisha and your boys." Don popped the holovid up again, showing Bryce's family together at the tram stop, his boys just home from school. "Your little woman gets a patron in the form of a civic-minded individual who wants to help a widow make ends meet—and then some. Your boys get tuition to private schools, so they can get nice, safe, respectable jobs. Not like the jobs you just left, or the jobs you and me got now. Whaddaya say?"

Bryce used to wonder about the sort of weak, petty men who got dragged into organized crime. He understood now. When it all came down to it, all that mattered was family. And

Bryce Brisson—or whatever his next alias would be—was willing to do anything for his.

"Deal."

Thanks for reading!

You made it to the end! Maybe you're just persistent, but hopefully that means you enjoyed the book. But this is just the end of one story. If you'd like reading my books, there are always more on the way!

Perks of being an Email Insider include:

- Notification of book releases (often with discounts)
- Inside track on beta reading
- Advance review copies (ARCs)
- Access to Inside Exclusive bonus extras and giveaways
- Best of my blog about fantasy, science fiction, and the art of worldbuilding

Sign up for the my Email Insiders list at: jsmorin.com/updates

Books by J.S. Morin

Black Ocean

Black Ocean is a fast-paced fantasy space opera series about the small crew of the *Mobius* trying to squeeze out a living. If you love fantasy and sci-fi, and still lament over the cancellation of *Firefly*, *Black Ocean* is the series for you!

Read about the Black Ocean series and discover where to buy at: blackoceanmissions.com

Twinborn Trilogy

Experience the journey of mundane scribe Kyrus Hinterdale who discovers what it means to be Twinborn—and the dangers of getting caught using magic in a world that thinks it exists only in children's stories.

Read about the *Twinborn Trilogy* and discover where to buy at: twinborntrilogy.com

Mad Tinker Chronicles

Then continue on into the world of Korr, where the Mad Tinker and his daughter try to save the humans from the oppressive race of Kuduks. When their war spills over into both Tellurak and Veydrus, what alliances will they need to forge to make sure the right side wins?

Read about the *Mad Tinker Chronicles* and discover where to buy at: madtinkerchronicles.com

About the Author

I am a creator of worlds and a destroyer of words. As a fantasy writer, my works range from traditional epics to futuristic fantasy with starships. I have worked as an unpaid Little League pitcher, a cashier, a student library aide, a factory grunt, a cubicle drone, and an engineer—there is some overlap in the last two.

Through it all, though, I was always a storyteller. Eventually I started writing books based on the stray stories in my head, and people kept telling me to write more of them. Now, that's all I do for a living.

I enjoy strategy, worldbuilding, and the fantasy author's privilege to make up words. I am a gamer, a joker, and a thinker of sideways thoughts. But I don't dance, can't sing, and my best artistic efforts fall short of your average notebook doodle. When you read my books, you are seeing me at my best.

My ultimate goal is to be both clever and right at the same time. I have it on good authority that I have yet to achieve it.

Connect with me online
On my blog at jsmorin.com
On Facebook at facebook.com/authorjsmorin
On Twitter at twitter.com/authorjsmorin

48023724R00107

Made in the USA
Lexington, KY
18 December 2015